THE BAYNES CLAN: NEVADA TOUGH

Also by John S. McCord in Large Print:

The Baynes Clan: The Montana Horseman
The Baynes Clan: Texas Comebacker

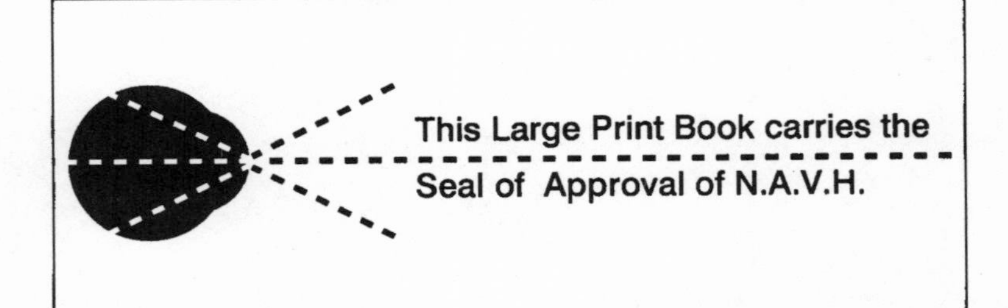

THE BAYNES CLAN: NEVADA TOUGH

JOHN S. MCCORD

All of the characters in this book except for certain historical figures are fictitious, and any resemblance to actual persons, living or dead, is purely coincidental.

Published in 2003 by arrangement with P.M.A. Literary and Film Management, Inc.

Wheeler Large Print Western Series.

The text of this Large Print edition is unabridged.
Other aspects of the book may vary from the original edition.

Set in 16 pt. Plantin by Christina S. Huff.

Printed in the United States on permanent paper.

Library of Congress Cataloging-in-Publication Data

McCord, John S.
Nevada tough / McCord, John S.
p. cm. — (The Baynes clan)
ISBN 1-58724-307-5 (lg. print : sc : alk. paper)
1. Baynes family (Fictitious characters) — Fiction. 2. Nevada — Fiction. 3. Large type books. I. Title.
PS3563.C34439 N48 2003
813′.54—dc21 2002028086

To Joan,
perfect bodyguard
for the long passage

National Association for Visually Handicapped
serving the partially seeing

As the Founder/CEO of NAVH, the only national health agency solely devoted to those who, although not totally blind, have an eye disease which could lead to serious visual impairment, I am pleased to recognize Thorndike Press* as one of the leading publishers in the large print field.

Founded in 1954 in San Francisco to prepare large print textbooks for partially seeing children, NAVH became the pioneer and standard setting agency in the preparation of large type.

Today, those publishers who meet our standards carry the prestigious "Seal of Approval" indicating high quality large print. We are delighted that Thorndike Press is one of the publishers whose titles meet these standards. We are also pleased to recognize the significant contribution Thorndike Press is making in this important and growing field.

Lorraine H. Marchi, L.H.D.
Founder/CEO
NAVH

* Thorndike Press encompasses the following imprints: Thorndike, Wheeler, Walker and Large Pr int Press.

Thanks to Peggy Draper, Director of the Lincoln County Library in Pioche, Nevada.

Thanks to Betty Yarbrough, Director; Sheila Williams, Assistant Director; and Mary Wilber, Reference Librarian of the Euless Public Library, Euless, Texas.

These modern-day trackers never quit a trail. Without helpful librarians, writers run out of breath and turn blue.

Affection to citizens of Pioche, Nevada, a town with a lurid, violent, funny, fascinating history and a great place to visit. I used, twisted, and tinkered with Pioche history in this book. The real story is too strong to swallow straight.

Sometimes truth, like even the best Scotch, needs watering down to make believable fiction.

ONE

"I think it's obtuse, to speak candidly." Joe Thackery eyed the inch-long ash on his cigar with distrust for a moment before he decided to knock it off in the ashtray beside his chair.

Darnell Baynes squirmed himself into a more comfortable position in his chair and smiled at his immaculate partner. Sporting his usual spotless white shirt topped with a collar starched stiff as an iron mule shoe, Thackery showed none of the qualities of a dangerous man. People frequently mistook Thackery for a harmless, albeit strict and humorless, minister of some kind of stern faith. Yet, Darnell knew him to be deadly in a manner only possible in rare individuals who combine utter fearlessness with iron self-control.

Acquaintances and business associates in the busy town of Sacramento in 1872 allowed themselves to be misled by Thackery's small stature and prim mannerisms. His obvious concern of the moment, that his spotless black suit might be marred by a bit of cigar ash, was but one example. Few noticed that he never buttoned his coat nor that his right hand seldom wandered far from the holstered pistol at his hip. Even those observant enough to notice that were probably misled.

Thackery was left-handed and preferred to use the weapon hidden in a custom-fitted shoulder holster under his right arm. Sacramento residents would probably laugh in disbelief if told that Thackery left two land-grabbing carpetbaggers ready for burial when he left his native Virginia. Darnell smiled at the thought of anyone in his right mind trying to steal anything important from Joseph Finnigan Thackery.

Thackery allowed a brow to rise. "You find my opinion amusing?"

"No. Pardon me. My mind wandered for a moment," Darnell tapped the stack of paper in front of him on the wide, gleaming desk and asked, "You don't smell anything?"

"Of course I do. An absolutely rotten profit-and-loss statement like that one stinks to high heaven, but why bother with it personally? It could be dangerous. Why not send in auditors and have the Pinkertons investigate? That fellow, what was his name? Fitzpatrick, that was it. When an important stockholder like Fitzpatrick goes poking around and gets himself shot, that might mean it's prudent to keep a safe distance."

"We invested a big chunk of money in that Nevada mine, Joe. One of my sons once said it isn't righteous to steal, and it's the devil's work to tempt men by allowing it."

Thackery blew smoke toward the ceiling. "Luke. That had to be Luke. He always likes to drink deep from the cup of righteousness before he shoots somebody. He'd rather give them a friendly beating. Given a choice, if I had to confront Luke, I'd prefer to be shot."

Darnell chuckled. "Yeah, you guessed the right boy."

"Let me remind you of half a dozen facts, Darnell. We recovered our investment months ago, so we've already lapped up a nice measure of cream. If that mine peters out, and that may be all that's happening, we have no cause to complain. There's no real evidence we're being cheated."

"That's only four or five facts." Darnell grinned into Thackery's stern gaze, knowing his partner hated to be interrupted or rushed when speaking.

Thackery ignored him and continued his slow, measured rate of speech. "You still have to learn how to act like a rich man. A moneyed man doesn't go snooping around in a potentially dangerous situation. He hires hungry young men who want to make a name for themselves. By doing so, he increases the confidence of his associates by showing he's smart enough to deserve wealth."

"You're the only associate who makes any difference. You already know I'm not smart."

Thackery raised a finger, a glint of humor in his hard gaze. "I'd like that to be my little secret.

Who knows? We might want to borrow money someday."

"I doubt it."

Joe Thackery actually smiled, but he rubbed his mouth and quickly got himself back under control. "The possibility does seem remote. I'll concede that."

"I'm leaving in the morning."

"Very well, Darnell, if you insist. I can see you're in the grip of your overdeveloped sense of adventure. I'll get one of our clerks to buy train tickets for us."

"You're not going. You need to stay here and run things. Besides, I'm not going by train. I've decided to ride."

"You want to go by horseback? Alone? What the devil for?"

"Adventure. And I need to lose an inch. Look at this." Darnell pointed to the shiny stripe on his belt that showed plainly he'd had to let it out a notch. "First time I've had to do that since I was twenty."

Thackery nodded. "Merely a symbol of prosperity. Shows you're becoming a man of substance."

"Merely a symbol of sloth. Shows I need to get out and about before I become old and helpless because of plain laziness."

"Nonsense. A man such as you approaches his prime at fifty-three. Your best years still lie ahead if you resist immature impulses to ride into adversity alone."

"Sometimes a man has an advantage when he rides alone."

"Darnell, listen to me. You've seen plenty of trouble. Lords knows we've seen enough of it together to last most men a lifetime. But you always rode with your sons before. That's about the same as riding with a company of seasoned cavalry. At least let me get Ward to ride with you. He'll welcome a little vacation anyway."

"My youngest son rides out of sight of your daughter and he comes down with an itch worse than a man who slept in poison ivy. Ward likes to stay close to home."

"If something happens to you, your sons will burn Pioche to the ground, plow the ashes, and sow salt. Nothing will grow there for a hundred years. Of course, nobody will notice. Nothing but sage grows in Nevada anyway."

"What will you do if something happens to me?"

"As an older and wiser man, I would try to fill the role of mature counselor with your sons, of course. I would advise them to use a coarse grade of salt to avoid unnecessary expense, and I would advise them to take no prisoners. I doubt there's an honest man in the whole state of Nevada, if you forget a few stray Mormons."

"I'm charmed."

"And I'd pray for you, even though I know of no scripture that implies your stupidity hinders salvation."

"Such praise causes me to blush and endure hot flashes."

Thackery leaned forward and blew gently on his cigar, sending flakes of ash drifting aimlessly in the still air. "This is ridiculous. You'll ride into the area, announce your name, and in five minutes every man within miles will hear about it. The Baynes name is too well known for you not to be noticed. If somebody's cheating us, they'll cover up until they get you killed. Then they'll go back to work."

"I already considered that. I'll just call myself Nevada Darnell. That way I'll always answer when somebody calls me by name, but the Baynes part won't be there to attract attention."

Joe Thackery made no response, but his steady gaze and indulgent expression spoke for him. He waited patiently to hear more.

"No point in going in and asking to see the books. This report," Darnell tapped the papers in front of him, "clearly indicates the bad news, but it doesn't explain what's causing the problem. I'll hang around and watch, take a job maybe, and listen to the miners. They'll know if anybody is high-grading our ore, but they won't report anything as long as their paycheck comes on time. Miners have no love for owners. But they'll whisper about it among themselves. If they're not in on it, they'll gab about it out of envy if nothing else."

"You going to tell your sons what you're doing?"

"Sure. I've already written to them."

"Any answer?"

"Too soon. Besides, Luke has a court to preside over in Wyoming, and Milt has a new son and a big ranch to look after in Texas."

Thackery's eyes met Darnell's for a long moment. Then he nodded slowly. "You hide it well, but I saw the wild streak in you the day I met you. It's so strong in you it passed on to your sons. No call to criticize a cougar when it doesn't act like a rabbit nor a man who acts true to his nature. It's your neck. Let's go eat."

After a meal consumed in almost perfect silence, Darnell said good night to his partner and strolled through the early spring evening to the spacious house he occupied alone. He locked the door behind him and wandered slowly through the beautifully furnished, spotless rooms, his footsteps echoing as if to mock him. The building, although graced with the appointments of wealth and good taste, sounded hollow, and the echoes fitted Darnell's black mood.

In the gathering dusk, he sat in one of the dining chairs and leaned forward, resting his elbows on the polished surface of the table. Long and shining, the table would seat ten. It stretched in front of him like a placid pool of water, reflecting the shadowy chandelier above and the curtained window at the far end of the room. The reflection showed no movement, like a pool without fish, frog, or insect, a dead pond.

Darnell had never lived in a house alone. He didn't find it lonely. He found it sad. A house had no chance to come alive, to become a home, without a woman burning food in the kitchen and children hurtling about playing games, starting fights, and breaking things. No carpet in this house had been chewed by a puppy. No chair leg carried scars from a growing boy who forgot to remove his spurs. He saw no clutter, nothing out of place.

He knew the house caused none of his uneasiness, but its spotless perfection emphasized his dull life. Darnell Baynes knew he suffered from pure and simple boredom. He'd worked desperately hard to make a place for himself, to court and win the perfect woman. Even after all the years, he felt the old flash of anger that she'd died. How could she? And then came the same old stab of shame for his selfishness. She hadn't chosen to die. She'd fought like a tigress to live, and the love in her eyes during the last moments still haunted him, still made his eyes water.

Now, he had three grown sons well started in lives of their own, and he had more money than he knew how to spend. And he had discovered that managing wealth, for him, had become the most boring labor imaginable.

What next? Was he finished, the only purpose left in his life to drift slowly into a jaded, lonely old age? Success should yield comfort, satisfaction, not bored yawning all day wondering why the hands on his watch seemed stuck.

Once before, when his spirited Spanish wife died, he'd felt like a bucket with no bottom. The juice of life drained out of him when he stood beside her grave. He'd taken to remote trails with his sons, never staying anywhere long enough to grow roots. Every day brought change, danger, new challenge.

Success had settled him in the mild climate of California, and emptiness, following relentlessly and never far behind, had finally caught up. Darnell now understood that the empty man must keep moving, keep facing danger or achingly difficult hard work. Otherwise, he had time to look inside — and find himself hollow. He wondered if a man who looked inside and found demons might be better off than one who found nothing.

TWO

Darnell awoke the morning after his first day on the trail and eyed his surroundings through slitted eyes before rising. Satisfied that all looked and sounded normal, he rolled out of his blankets, strapped on the Navy Colt .36, slapped on his hat, and jerked on his boots. Then he stretched cautiously and allowed himself a grin of pleasure when he found no stiffness.

Not bad for an old man. He'd decided to take it easy on himself, only covering a sedate twenty miles the first day out. Still, he'd walked half and ridden half, and he felt a smug touch of satisfaction. He'd felt no fatigue yesterday nor did he feel any sore spots today. His trousers felt loose, so he jerked his belt a notch tighter, back to the old adjustment. Magic. He'd lost the extra inch he'd complained about to Thackery in one day. Maybe a short spell of town living hadn't clipped his fighting spurs and turned him into a plump and soft old bird after all.

One match started the kindling under the coffee pot, and he turned to saddle his mount and tie the pack to his second horse. By the time he returned to the fire, the water simmered nicely, so he dropped in a careless handful of coffee and put sliced bacon into the frying pan. Thirty minutes after waking, he swung into the saddle, rode the half mile back to the trail, and turned his face to the first rays of the rising sun.

Old habits ruled him. By abiding custom, he never camped overnight near where he cooked his evening meal or near any fire site unless forced to it by bitter cold, and he never slept close to a traveled road or near water. In the mornings, he rode away before the smell of frying bacon or hot coffee could drift very far downwind to catch the attention of the curious. To do otherwise invited company, and cautious men who survived travel in empty country retained little sense of hospitality. Empty country could turn dangerous quicker than a man could blink when strangers came together.

He rode with a smug smile pasted on his face, feeling like a frolicsome puppy trotting away from a slipped leash. Riding straight at trouble offered the greatest cure for boredom in the world, and it surely proved him to be infected with a lingering immaturity if not actual craziness. His smile widened when he felt a rush of warm kinship and affection for his middle son. Milton would understand and agree with this foolhardy plan, would jump to come along if he had the chance, would start saddling quickly in fear he might be left behind. From time to time, when things seemed too peaceful, Milt showed a partiality to stir the pot, just for fun.

Milt had astonished his brothers one day: After having pinned down the Baynes clan in a buffalo wallow for three days, a Comanche war party broke off the fight. The young fool sprang to his feet, ran toward the departing warriors, and shouted in Spanish, "Come back here, women! We're not through fighting yet." The departing warriors heard and turned back, but all they did was gallop back and forth beyond firing range, riding high on their mustang ponies, and slapping their bare buttocks in derision. Milt looked sadly at his dead horse and muttered, "Damn, I can't even chase 'em."

Luke, his oldest son, had looked at Darnell and shaken his head in disgust. "Pa, one of your sons has less brains than a chicken."

Darnell realized how dense he'd been all these years not to have grasped the fact that Milt came by his foolhardy actions honestly. He got it from his father. Darnell, with all his cautious ways, had always thought of the safety of his sons first. Now, riding without them, he felt like Milt. Riding alone set a man free from concerns about others, allowed his tendency to spit in the devil's eye to come to the surface. A man never felt so alive as when riding into danger. Every leaf turned greener, every sunrise brighter, every breath sweeter, every sound clearer. The call to battle caused even gray old war horses to prance, eyes bright and ears pricked.

He rode slowly and walked often, feeling no sense of haste, simply letting the days slip past.

The ground sloped gradually as he approached the high Sierras, and the April warmth cooled as he neared Carson Pass. His chosen route wasn't an easy one, but he wanted to cross into Nevada south of Reno and Virginia City. On the third day out, he rode past a stage station, pulled his horse to a halt, and considered. Finally, he decided to act sensible and ask if the pass was still snowbound. Besides, a meal he didn't cook himself might be a welcome change. He turned back.

Three horses stood hipshot at the hitching rail when he dismounted, the noon sun throwing shadows directly under the motionless animals. Darnell resisted the impulse to raise an eyebrow, and deliberately avoided looking at the horses too closely. It took no more than a roving glance to see that these were no ordinary mounts. Horseflesh of this quality either meant that the riders inside were men of substance who could afford the best, or it signaled that they depended on fast transportation to stay alive. A fast horse had more value to a knowing outlaw than a fast gun, and a man who examined horses too closely could easily be mistaken for a lawman on the hunt.

The door stood wide open, and Darnell slipped in and to the side, away from the doorway. Three men sat on a crude bench to his right behind the only table in the spacious room. They sat with their backs against the log wall. Another man stood behind the rough plank bar to the left. A blanket hung across a doorway at the far end of the room, directly across from the front door.

The man behind the bar said, "Come in, sir. Lunch is almost ready. You're just in time."

Darnell caught an undertone of relief in the man's voice and noted the friendly smile on a square-jawed open face. He nodded. "That sounds good. Doesn't take a man long to get tired of his own cooking."

One of the other men, tall and painfully thin, said, "This here table ain't big enough for four. Wait till we're through, old man."

Darnell eased over to the bar and leaned his left elbow on the rough surface. The three seated men sat up straighter when he brushed his coat back from the Navy at his hip. His gaze slid down the long table that could seat eight. With the three men all sitting with their backs to the wall, the entire bench on the near side of the table stood empty. "That'll be fine. I'm in no hurry."

The skinny face split into a wide grin revealing a row of yellow teeth. "Hear that, fellers? He ain't in no hurry." He elbowed the man next to him and chortled, "He ain't in no hurry," again as if it were the punch line for a big joke.

The other two men, older and shorter, exchanged glances. One of them shifted his attention to Darnell and shook his head, an almost invisible movement.

A young girl, probably in her mid-teens,

brushed aside the blanket covering the doorway and carried a stack of plates and cutlery to the table. She nodded to Darnell. "I didn't know you were here. Do you want to eat, sir?"

"Never mind him, sweety. He'll eat our leavings." The lanky hardcase leaned forward and around the end of the table and grabbed her dress at the hip. "No rush. Why don't you sit on my lap for awhile?"

She slapped at his hand, but he pulled her toward him. The man came from behind the bar, stepped forward, and said, "Here, here now, stop that. She's my daughter."

The lanky man shoved the girl away and came to his feet, right hand hovering over the gun at his hip. The bartender, caught in the middle of the room, halted and took a step back, hands lifted in front of him. "What's the matter with you, fellow? I'm not even armed."

When the girl sent a desperate glance at him, Darnell said, "Go back to the kitchen and stay there."

Everyone in the room except the girl looked at Darnell as if surprised to find him still there, as if they had forgotten him. "Go back to the kitchen," he said again. "This man's thinking about leaving. While he's working it out, stay out of his way. Thinking's hard for him." His eyes fixed on the crouched man, he added, "You two put your hands on the table, please."

The other two men instantly understood that he spoke to them and placed their hands on the table. One said, "We aren't in this." Darnell found the remark unnecessary. The flattened hands spoke for them more clearly than words.

"I figured you looked too smart for that. What's this idiot's name?"

"I'm Stretch Cozart, old man. I guess you've heard of me." When Darnell didn't reply, Cozart's smirk tightened with irritation. "You had a chance to shut up and clear out of here, but I'm not sure I'll let you walk away now. I ain't partial to being called an idiot by doddering old fools." The longfingered hand hovering over the holstered pistol had turned into a claw, and the stringy frame tightened like a bow string. The man trembled with eagerness, a vacant smile pasted on his lips. Without looking at the girl or her father, he said, "Go on out of here. I'll call you when I finish with this old dimwit."

The girl backed into the kitchen, but her father retreated to his position behind the bar.

Darnell found himself smiling. This senseless argument fitted his reckless mood, and he felt the old, familiar tightening somewhere in the center of him. He faked a kindly voice. "No, I haven't heard of you, Retch. I knew a Taterhead Cozart years ago, and you sort of favor him. He was bony, awkward, and stupid like you. Had a long bald head just like a potato. I heard some Mexicans hanged him down south for stealing chickens. But don't worry about it. You'll probably be fairly famous after today."

"Oh, yeah? Why's that?"

"You'll be added to a long list of dead morons, but you'll be the first one who stood up and asked Darnell Baynes to kill him." Darnell noted with cynical satisfaction the impact of his name. The rail-thin gunman's mouth twitched, and a sparse flicker of his eyes reflected the jolt.

"You ain't Darnell Baynes. You ain't old enough. He must be over sixty years old by now. I ain't falling for that dodge."

From behind the bar, the bartender spoke, his voice dripping satisfaction.

"He's Darnell Baynes all right. I was tending bar in Montana a few years back, and I saw him in good light one night. He brought in one of his boys to get a bullet crease on his cheek sewed up. That boy, Ward was his name, sat there like a stone statue while the doctor sewed up that wound.

"That kid didn't look over fifteen or sixteen years old, but he had the coldest ways about him I ever saw. Young fellow could give you chilblains just by looking at you. He married the prettiest girl you ever saw, though, right there in that saloon, with rags soaked with his blood still lying all over a table. The Baynes clan killed three or four men the very day that kid got married. Didn't mean a thing to them. Acted like it was just another ordinary day. I'll testify they ain't the kind of folks a body forgets."

The lanky gunfighter snarled, "Shut up. You chatter worse than a woman, barkeep." His body tilted forward and his vacant, fake grin faded. He took a couple of stiff-legged steps forward, coming to a halt in front of the kitchen doorway. Now only about ten feet separated him from Darnell. "If you're Baynes, I'm the one to drop you. I ain't scared of no man with a rusty rep. You want to try for that gun, old man, or you gonna just stand there while I shoot you?"

Darnell's attention narrowed to a tight focus. He felt the inner stillness of a quiet, malignantly cold concentration for the first time in years, and he welcomed it. All hesitation, all doubt fled. The man in front of him would fall, whatever else happened, whether he had to take lead himself or not.

He felt sure the other two, sitting breathlessly still with their hands flat on the table in front of them, wanted no part of this pointless argument. He waited for Cozart to make his move, watching the man's whole body, waiting for a telltale shift of weight, tilt of a shoulder, or any of the potential hints that almost always come a split second before the gun hand moves.

When Cozart took those two steps forward, he sent a message as clearly as if he'd spoken. The man wanted to be close, confident of his quickness, less sure of his accuracy. Darnell took a step forward himself, and watched Cozart's eyes widen with shock. Now they stood so close, with less than six feet separating them, nobody could miss. Getting close was one thing, but getting too close was next door to suicide.

Cozart's thin face began to quiver with tension. Unable to stand the pressure, he took a couple of steps back.

From the corner of his eye, Darnell caught a flicker of movement at the kitchen doorway. Nerves set on a hair trigger to react to any movement, he exploded into action, bringing his Navy up and cocked, but he didn't fire. A sheet of water struck the lanky Cozart with a sloppy splat. His upper body vanished for a second in the cloud of water and steam that sloshed across his face and against his right side from hat to hip. The force of the gush of liquid knocked off his sweat-stained Stetson.

Both the astonished gunman's arms sprang up in a futile attempt to shield his scalded eyes as he tried to duck away, instinctively but too late, from the blistering torrent. His mouth an open testament to surprise and searing pain, he gasped and pawed frantically at his eyes, his face caught in a frame of rising steam. Then his high-pitched shriek seemed to unlock his joints as he crumpled to his knees, head bowed into twitching hands. He never saw the iron kettle the young woman swung in a wide, relentless arc. Darnell's left hand sprang up in a sympathetic defensive gesture, and he gave an involuntary grunt of his own when the black kettle struck the gunman's head with a grisly but oddly musical bass thump.

Frozen in astonishment, Darnell saw the

young woman shift her feet in what seemed an unhurried, graceful transferral of balance, a smooth dance step to set her weight perfectly for the next swing. Yet, she moved so quickly he had no chance to hinder her. He realized he still stood with his left hand lifted in forgotten gesture and his right holding his cocked and leveled Navy.

Cozart, now sitting in slack, stunned immobility from the first blow, hands resting palms up in his lap, caught the second square in the face. No musical clang came this time.

The brittle, gritty crunch caused the hair at Darnell's collar to bristle and the muscles of his chest and stomach to tighten in an involuntary flinch. He dropped his left arm, still raised in a reflex move, and holstered the Navy.

Cozart fell over backward. His boots, awkwardly trapped under his buttocks, prevented his legs from straightening. Lying with his spine cruelly arched backward and with his legs folded back under him so strangely, he appeared to have been cut off at the knees. Then he seemed to snap back to consciousness. He shifted to free his feet so his legs could straighten, gave a bubbling sob, and blindly reached for his gun.

The concussion of a shotgun blast from behind the bar struck at Darnell like simultaneous blows to each ear. His head ached and rang and he jerked up an elbow and ducked in defense against a second blast as the bartender leaned forward to line the shotgun at the bloody mess on the floor. His finger slowly relaxed on the second trigger of the double-barreled ten-gauge.

After four or five seconds of utter silence, the bartender eased the second hammer of the shotgun down. "I guess there's no need to waste powder. He looks comfortable enough."

Surprised that he could still hear anything, Darnell shook his head and rubbed both ears. He glanced at his hands and felt a rush of relief when he saw no blood. "Man, that thing made us all deaf. We'll have a headache for a month. I'll bet you lifted shingles off the roof."

The bartender laid the shotgun across the bar and waved a hand in front of his face to clear away some of the smoke that filled the room. He reached down and shook a gun belt out of its coil around a holstered pistol. As soon as he slapped it around his waist and buckled it, he looked at Darnell through shaggy brows. "First time I took this off in twenty years except to go to bed, and look what happened."

Darnell worked a finger into an ear and shook his head again. He stepped across the room and stared down at the rough circle of blood in the center of Cozart's crushed chest. "You usually wear a gun behind the bar?"

"It's been a comfort, time to time. Things been so quiet around here of late, I got careless." He shook his head. "Man with a full-grown daughter oughtn't to get neglectful. All kinds of trashy pilgrims drift through here."

One of the men sitting like statues behind the table coughed and lowered his hands from his ears. When Darnell met his gaze, he asked, "Mr. Baynes, I wonder if my brother and I can step outside till the smoke clears? We just met that fellow on the trail this morning. We never had any reason to suspect he was a fugitive from a madhouse."

The bartender didn't raise his eyes from the shotgun while he reloaded. "Mr. Baynes, I'm Joshua Prime. This here," he nodded toward the two men as they rose slowly to their feet, "is Mr. Moses Perlman on the left and Mr. Timothy Perlman on the right. The Perlman brothers own the stage line that comes through here three times a week. I work for them, and they're the best bosses I ever had." He slid the shotgun back under the bar and turned to the girl. "Miss Ruth Prime, may I present Mr. Darnell Baynes. Mr. Baynes, meet my daughter Ruth."

Darnell jerked off his hat and bowed. The girl curtsied as prettily as ever he'd seen it done. She looked pale and round-eyed but perfectly composed, still holding an empty iron kettle that looked too big for her to lift and standing a step away from a bloody corpse in a room filled with eye-stinging powder smoke. The youngster stood her ground, shoulders squared, jaw set, feet planted with the same haughty determination as a Spanish matador.

The Perlman brothers came around the table.

The tallest said, "I'm Moses." The other, almost an echo, said, "I'm Timothy." Darnell slapped his hat back on and shook hands with each in turn.

Prime hitched up his belt and stepped around the bar. "Take a good look and don't mix them two up. They get fussed over being mistaken for each other. I keep telling them that all Jews look alike, but they don't take kindly to the notion."

Chuckling from his crude attempt at humor, he stooped to explore Cozart's pockets and grunted in disgust. "Might have known. Nothing to tell if he's got family somewhere or anything like that. Poor fool probably couldn't read, so nobody sent him letters or such." He clicked a few coins from the man's poke like dice in his hand for a second or two, shrugged, and pocketed them. "Burial expenses."

When he glanced around the room and nobody answered, he stepped between Cozart's legs, bent over, and grabbed the heels of the dead man's boots. Then he dragged the body toward the front door like a man pulling a wheelbarrow. "Now I got to dig a deep hole. I hate digging, but he had nearly twenty dollars, so I got to do right by him. Nobody can claim that Joshua Prime ever poured a short measure." He passed out the front door without a backward glance, grumbling with every step.

Ruth glanced at the bloody streaks and splatters on the plank floor and turned toward the kitchen.

Moses Perlman said flatly, "Leave it."

She paused. At her questioning look, he added, "I have a man coming to replace your father, Miss Prime. He'll be here in an hour or two. You might as well start packing."

For the first time, Darnell saw her look shaken. She slowly lowered the kettle and a hand rose to trembling lips. "You aren't going to fire my father, are you, Mr. Perlman? This wasn't his fault. He works so hard, and he really needs this job, sir. He says he never worked for better bosses. I know he has an awful sense of humor, but he really admires both of you. Please don't fire him."

Timothy Perlman lifted a hand, and her gaze snapped to him. "Now, now, Miss Prime. You mustn't fret. Far from firing your father, we need him badly. Honest, hardworking men like him are almost impossible to find these days. We need to replace one of our managers. My brother and I want him to take charge of a freight office and livery yard. He'll make twice as much with all that new responsibility, and he'll get to live in town. You wouldn't mind living in town, would you?"

Ruth took a deep breath and sighed. "Mr. Perlman, you scared me to death for a minute there. Does he know?"

Timothy shrugged and smiled. "I'm surprised to hear anything could frighten you, Miss Prime. And no, ma'am, he doesn't know yet. We thought we'd break the news after we had a pleasant lunch. Your cooking has caused a bit of talk up and down the line. We'll hate to lose that advantage, but we heard Joshua say he wished he could find a place where you could get some more schooling. You wouldn't mind that either, would you?"

She smiled, her expression changing in an instant from that of a rigidly controlled young woman to a delighted child on Christmas morning. Her feet shifted two or three times before Darnell realized she was fighting to keep from dancing with joy.

"Can I go tell him?"

Timothy Perlman looked at his brother. The two seemed to be able to communicate without speech. Moses spoke slowly, "We think you might do that, Miss Prime, but there's a proper time for these things."

"Proper time?"

"Yes, ma'am. Seems to us your father would welcome the news after he's had time to enjoy his grumbling and griping over having to dig a deep hole."

She clapped her hands and giggled. "He'll be flummoxed. Purely staggered. It'll be wonderful." Then, as if struck by a thought, she paused. "Where? Where are we going?"

"Over into Nevada, young lady. Your daddy will be taking you to Pioche."

"Pioche? Where in the world is that?"

"Down in the south part of the Great Basin, ma'am. It's an awful place, but it is a town. It won't be as lonely for you as this isolated station." Moses Perlman's kindly tone hinted at why the crusty Prime spoke of him and his brother as being good bosses. He turned to Darnell. "Why don't we step outside and let the smoke clear, Mr. Baynes?"

THREE

Watching Joshua Prime dig a grave for the body carelessly tossed to the side, Darnell asked, "Who's the law around here?"

Prime straightened and leaned against the shovel. "Ain't none."

"None?"

Prime pulled a rag from his pocket and mopped his face. "Well, there's a marshal back down the road yonder way about fifty miles. Rough traveling. Take about a day and a half to get there unless a man planned to risk ruining his horse. Ain't no concern. The Perlman boys will let him know what happened. They saw it and all that. The Perlmans are big men in these parts. Won't be no questions asked." Prime spoke as if the two Perlmans were not standing beside Darnell and hearing every word.

Darnell extended a hand toward the shovel. "I might as well help, since I'm just standing around anyway."

"Obliged, but I'll handle it. I been paid for the work, in a way of speaking."

"No trouble for me to help. You can keep the money."

Prime shook his head and kicked the blade

into the loosened soil at the bottom of the hole. "You might mention to the Perlmans, just a casual remark, that you being here don't add nothing to the story of what happened to this fellow."

Darnell stood silent, staring off into the distance.

Continuing to ignore the fact that the brothers stood only four or five feet from him, Prime continued, "If a man happened to be on the dodge, and having his name brought up would cause problems, the Perlman boys understand that there ain't no profit in causing trouble. They mind their own business. Good men."

"I'm not on the dodge, but that sounds like good advice. I think I might have a word with them."

Prime nodded without looking up. "No offense."

"None taken. It's just that my so-called reputation won't be helped by having what happened here get around."

Prime stopped work and looked up with a questioning expression. "How do you figure that? If you ain't on the dodge, where's the grievance? You didn't do nothing wrong."

"It's just I don't want it talked around that a wee bit of a girl was faster with a kettle of hot water than I was with a pistol."

Prime laughed, but quickly sobered. "Now that's a thought, ain't it, Mr. Baynes? Thinking deeper on that idea, it won't do that little scrap of a girl no credit neither. Once a man has time to ponder on it, that story wouldn't make her sound like she was acting the proper lady, not even close."

Careful not to glance at the brothers, Darnell copied Joshua Prime's pretense. "Seems to me the story holds up fine with Stretch yonder getting a skin full of whiskey, going hog-wild out of control, and trying to throw down on a bartender who happened to have a shotgun handy. Won't be the first time in the world that kind of thing happened. No need to lie about it, if leaving out part of the story doesn't count for lying. No big reason for either the girl or me to get mentioned."

Moses Perlman turned to his brother. "Can you see me?"

Timothy nodded. "Quite clearly."

"I can see you too. We're standing right here, aren't we, both of us? Why can't these two gentiles see us?"

"They're pretending, brother. It's a primitive ruse to get us to volunteer to do what they want without them having to ask. They're afraid they'll suffer from gas and constipation if they have to ask a favor of anybody."

Moses nodded. "Convenient, brother, but it's only fair if it works both ways. We can discuss it as if they aren't here either. All they're asking us to do is commit perjury. Such a small thing."

Timothy nodded in return. "Yes, that's all.

Thank heaven it's nothing difficult or important."

Moses added, "Or necessary."

Prime looked up. "What's that?"

Moses Perlman asked in a shocked tone. "You heard me? Can you see me too?"

Prime waved an impatient hand. "Why not necessary?"

Moses squatted comfortably by the deepening grave. "It might be better for you to escape across the border into Nevada, Joshua." He glanced over his shoulder at Darnell and winked. "You weren't directly involved, Mr. Baynes. Unlike Joshua here, unless you're already a fugitive, you have no need to flee."

"That's right," Tim said, face set in stern lines. "Even if Joshua Prime is tried and found not guilty, it wouldn't be good business for us to keep a man out here who shoots customers. It would be wise for him to head across the closest state line right away."

Moses Perlman added, "The marshal is a decent man. He is also a man of discretion who only tells people what he thinks they have a right to know. However, I've heard rumors that he shows an evil temper when people lie to him. I think it best we tell the truth, all of it."

Prime's face tensed for a moment, and he stood still in the grave. Then he nodded slowly and went back to digging. "You men know best. I never stayed around and hurt the business of anybody I ever worked for. I ain't that kind. Me and Ruth, we'll be moving on soon's you can get somebody out here to take my place."

Moses Perlman rubbed his chin for a moment as if in deep thought. "Surely, that'll be best. We have a man coming. He should be here any minute."

Prime straightened and leaned against the shovel. "You already got a new man hired? Now ain't I the fool? I thought I done good work here. How come you men planned to run me off?"

Darnell excused himself and walked back toward the stage station so the Perlman brothers could break the news of Prime's promotion to him in private. They had evidently decided not to wait for Ruth to tell her father. When he entered, Ruth stood beside the bloody spots on the floor, a bucket of water standing by. She glanced at him and said, "My daddy's boss said to leave this be, but I ought to clean things up, seems to me. The new man shouldn't have to do this. This isn't his mess."

Darnell picked up the mop she had leaned against the wall and plunged it into the water. He stopped when he saw steam rising from the mop. "Ma'am, you don't want to use hot water to clean up blood. It sets the stain. If you'll show me the well, I'll draw some cool water and clean this up. That way you don't get in trouble, and the new man doesn't have a mess to clean up his first day on the job."

"Not your mess either, Mr. Baynes."

"No, but I don't work for the Perlman brothers, so I don't have to worry about orders they give."

She darted behind the curtain and reappeared a few seconds later with another bucket of water. After watching him swab the floor for a moment, she asked, "How did you learn so much about cleaning up blood stains, sir?"

"I once had a wife to teach me useful things, Miss Prime. We had three sons who managed to get banged up now and then. She was about the smartest woman in the world, I guess. Knew three languages, could recite poetry by the hour, and kept a neat house." He straightened to squeeze the mop into the bucket. "And she knew how to look after a husband and three boys and make it look easy."

"People make things they love to do look easy, don't you think, Mr. Baynes?"

"I don't mean to be nosy, Miss Prime, but would you take offense if I asked how old you are?"

"No, sir. I'm nineteen. Why?"

"I took you for younger, but your last remark sounded mighty grown up for as young as I thought you were."

She sighed. "Everybody takes me for half grown."

"My youngest son has the same trouble. It irritates him."

"I saw him."

"You saw Ward?"

"Yes, sir. Daddy and I were in Sacramento one time. He pointed Ward out to me on the street, and told his story about watching the doctor work on him up in Montana. I think that scar on his cheek makes him even better looking. I got a little breathless until I saw his wife. No proper woman would try for a married man, but seeing Ward's wife would discourage her if she was tempted. Nobody would have a chance against a woman that pretty. Are all your sons as good-looking as Ward?"

Darnell smiled. "Thank you, Miss Prime. All my boys are presentable, and they married lovely women if I'm any judge."

She nodded and said in a matter-of-fact tone, "All the nice ones get married before I ever see them."

"Not me. I'm nice. You interested in old widowers?"

"Now stop your teasing, Mr. Baynes. I suppose you're trying to take my mind off all this trouble. That's kind of you." She picked up the bucket of bloody water and smiled at him. "Besides, you're not too old for anybody but me, Mr. Baynes. I've made up my mind to catch a young man before he learns all the vices."

"I guess I am riddled with vices, Miss Prime, now that you mention it. Men fall prey to their favorite sins quickly in life. You better settle for a young man with a few mild faults unless you want to ask a ten-year-old to support you."

"Now it's my turn."

"Your turn?" Darnell straightened, wondering what on earth she was talking about.

"Yes, sir. I didn't get offended when you asked how old I am, did I?"

"No, ma'am."

"Then you owe me one."

"I guess you mean I owe you an impertinent question."

"Yes, sir."

"That's fair. I guess it should teach me not to be so nosy. All right, ask your question."

"Why don't you shave off your beard?"

"I beg your pardon?"

"I said, why don't you shave off your beard? All that gray in your beard makes you look older. Take off your hat."

Darnell removed his hat and felt an utter fool, standing like a post while she circled him.

"Just like I thought. You hardly have any gray in your hair. You should shave. Then, instead of looking like a man who's a whole lot too old for me, you'll look like a man who's just a little bit too old."

He jammed his Stetson back on his head. "Young lady, you punish a man hard for asking personal questions. You raise the ante mighty fast when you take your turn."

"I answered your question, Mr. Baynes. You didn't answer mine. You changed the subject. Do you think that's fair?"

Darnell couldn't decide whether to lose patience with this young woman or laugh. She stood with the bucket hanging from her hand like she was ready to wait all day for his answer. He thought he might try to jolt her a bit. "If you'll bring me some hot water, I'll shave right now."

"Done." She turned toward the kitchen.

"Wait."

Ruth paused in the opening, hand on the blanket.

"I don't need hot water as badly as Cozart. No throwing, please. Just bring it and hand it to me."

She giggled and swung the bucket in mock threat.

Joshua Prime stomped in, followed by the smiling Perlman brothers. "Ruth, how would you like to go to Nevada?"

"I'll have our wagon packed by sundown, Daddy. We can start tomorrow."

"Well now, that was quick. No pondering or head scratching at all. We're going to Pioche, daughter, one of the wildest, meanest towns in the world."

"I know." She disappeared behind the blanket.

"Everybody knows everything except me here lately." Prime looked at Darnell through bushy brows. "We'll be taking the shortest way, heading up through Carson Pass. Still lots of snow up there. Might be a little chancy if the weather turns sour. Might could use some company. Were you heading that way, Mr. Baynes?"

Darnell stood silently for a moment, mind

racing. He certainly didn't consider himself in a galloping hurry else he would have taken a train, but he didn't favor slowing down to wagon speed either. On the other hand, he'd taken a liking to the square-shouldered Prime and his plain-spoken daughter. That "might could use some company" probably came as close to an open plea for assistance this fellow could muster.

Why not tag along with them? Making a friend of the man who'd be running the biggest freight stage line in town might be handy. Perlman and Perlman did the ore hauling for the Raymond and Ely Mine, in which Darnell and Joe Thackery held their block of stock. If someone was high-grading ore, Joshua Prime's teamsters might be the best source of information available. This might turn into a stroke of luck worthy of a gambler's dream. "Fact is I'm heading for Pioche myself. We could ride along together if you'd like company."

Joshua Prime stuck out his hand. When Darnell grasped the callused hand, Prime grinned. "Be a pleasure to find out the real truth behind all the stories I've heard about you all these years. The rumor I hear most often here lately is that the Baynes boys have all settled down."

"That's not a rumor. That's the truth." Darnell met Prime's grin with a smile of his own.

"Last I heard, everybody agrees the reason for it is that your family done run plumb out of enemies. Looking forward to riding with you, Mr.

Baynes. I figure a man who has buried all his enemies should be interesting company."

Darnell shook his head and said slowly, "A man who doesn't make enemies has more to admire about him than one who buries them."

"Fine and dandy. The tales I've heard about you and your boys would curl the hair on a grizzly, Mr. Baynes. You know the one thing, seems to me, all of those windies have in common?"

Darnell shook his head again.

"A Baynes makes the best friend and the most dangerous enemy a man could have. That ain't such a bad thing to have floating down the wind. A man could put up with worse talk than that."

Moses Perlman walked behind the bar and poured himself a drink. He lifted the bottle toward his brother and got a nod. As soon as he'd sloshed whiskey into three more glasses, he looked at Darnell and Prime, pointed at one of the glasses and then another. "Since we had a shooting and a burying instead of dinner, we might as well have a drink while we wait for supper."

Ruth's raised voice reached them from the kitchen. "I can put dinner on the table if you men are hungry. I didn't let anything burn."

Moses turned to Prime, lifted his glass, and tossed down his drink. He spoke in a low tone. "That doesn't surprise me. I don't think an Indian attack would disturb your daughter, Mr.

Prime. She's a remarkably coolheaded young woman."

Prime shrugged and reached for one of the waiting drinks. "Runs in the family. Besides, she's seen more trouble than she ought. Girls without a mother and with a father who's got no learning have to look things in the eye. Life can be hard for poor folks. You men hungry?" When they all shook their heads, he spoke in a loud voice. "We'll just get by on spirits till supper, honey. You go ahead and eat if you're hungry."

Timothy Perlman turned to Darnell. "Mr. Baynes, I mean no offense, but I'd like to ask you a question."

"Go ahead. If I don't like the question, I won't answer it."

"Somehow, when you came in the door, I felt you were acting very cautious. Were you expecting trouble?"

"Not particularly, but I saw three fast horses outside. I figured that meant three wealthy men or three outlaws. When I saw you two, I took you for town men." He glanced at one brother and then the other. "Expensive city clothes, pale faces."

When both brothers nodded, Darnell continued. "Cozart didn't fit. I took him for your hired hand. I expected one or both of you to call him down and get him to behave. When you didn't, it still never came to me that you weren't together until after it was all over. I expected to have to shoot all three of you."

FOUR

The new man arrived on schedule, and Prime showed him around that evening. The Perlman brothers produced an inventory list and required the new man to acknowledge every piece of equipment at the stage station. They stated their intention to meet Joshua Prime in Pioche, but neither of them wanted anything to do with making the trip with him through Carson Pass. The Perlmans also settled the unspoken question about Cozart's horse by volunteering to turn the animal over to the law for disposition.

Ruth Prime made good her promise to have her father's wagon loaded and ready to roll before first light the next morning. She served breakfast, insisted that the new man inspect her clean kitchen, and climbed onto the wagon seat before Darnell finished saddling. Prime and his daughter waited patiently for Darnell to hitch his pack horse to the tailgate.

Darnell rode silently beside the wagon, enjoying the early morning light. Finally, he asked, "Why didn't you go with the Perlmans? You'd have to go the long way around, but the ride on the train would have been faster and easier."

Joshua Prime looked away and spat at the wagon wheel on the off side. "I read one time that trains go so fast they can put a strain on a person's organs, especially females. Man with a daughter can't take no chances."

Ruth, seated on the near side of the wagon seat, looked up at Darnell and smiled. After a long pause made it plain that her father had no intention of saying more, she said, "Trains make my daddy seasick." She sat comfortably, swaying with the motion of the wagon, looking straight forward and ignoring the disgusted glare from her father. Her gaze rose to meet Darnell's. "It's my turn again."

"I beg your pardon?"

"We answered your question. Now you owe us one."

Darnell settled back in the saddle. "I'm fast learning not to ask questions around your daughter."

Prime snorted. "Don't take long to get careful around her. No telling what she's likely to come out with."

She ignored both comments. "Deal?"

Darnell rubbed his newly shaved chin and nodded. "All right. I guess that's fair."

"I presume you aren't just riding around the country looking for ladies to save from men like Cozart."

"Only very pretty ladies. Was that a question?"

"No, that was an opinion. The question is, why are you going to Pioche?"

"Ain't none of your business, girl." Prime shifted restlessly on the wagon seat and shook his head.

"I have business affairs there."

"What business?"

"I'm learning to keep count. That's another question."

"No, it's not. It's a signal that you didn't really answer me. You didn't say anything but sidestep words. You dodged and looked smug. That's cheating."

Prime looked glum and sighed. "It ain't just you, Mr. Baynes. She's slow learning respect for men in general. Just ignore her and let it pass. That's what I do."

Darnell rode for a while scanning the trail ahead and thinking fast. The girl had given him a perfect opening. If he planned to get Prime's help, he'd need to level with the man sooner or later. Why not take advantage of this opportunity to deal honestly with him from the start? He grinned when his own frequently repeated joke to his sons came back to him. He'd often told them, "When all else fails, boys, tell the truth."

"I'm in partnership with a man named Joe Thackery. We own a chunk of stock in the Raymond and Ely Mine in Pioche. The profits started disappearing, and I want to snoop around and find out if we're getting cheated."

Prime's head snapped up, and he straightened in the wagon. "I remember that Thackery feller.

Father to that pretty girl your boy married, wasn't he? You was partnered with him in that gold mine up in Montana back in '67."

"Yeah. We got our start together up there and made a little money. I guess we're partners and family both now."

Prime's eyes narrowed and he frowned. "We do a lot of business with that mine. The Perlman brothers told me to take care not to cause no trouble with that account. Biggest customer we have."

"I wouldn't ask you to cause trouble, but I'd be obliged if you'd keep your ears open. Thackery and I own about twenty percent of that mine. A fellow named Fitzpatrick owned a little over twenty-five percent, and he got himself shot in Pioche a few months ago, just about the time the profits started downhill. William H. Raymond and John Ely, the men the mine's named after, own about thirty percent with the rest in the hands of small investors."

Prime nodded. "How come Raymond and Ely didn't keep ownership to themselves?"

"Owning a silver mine doesn't mean much unless you have the money to develop it, hire miners, pay freight, and all that. Poor men prospect and discover. Rich men invest and develop."

"Rich and poor got to work together, eh?"

"That's about it."

"And you got to be one of the rich ones with that strike up in Montana?"

"Yeah."

"Fitzpatrick got shot, you say? He die from it?"

"Yeah."

"Uh-huh." Prime spat at the wheel again. "Some thieves is more dangerous than others. Who got Fitzpatrick's stock?"

"I don't know yet."

"Uh-huh. You planning to find out and make them an offer?"

"Hadn't planned on it. Some folks pass around rumors about a mine failing to drive the price of stock down. When people get scared and willing to sell out cheap, they jump in and buy. Or, if a mine's really failing, they do the opposite and sell worthless stock for a high price. TBI doesn't work that way."

"TBI?"

"Thackery and Baynes Investments."

"Uh-huh. Well, I heard the Baynes clan done come up in the world. Me and Ruth saw that fancy house of yours when we was in Sacramento. You're doing mighty fine for a man with an outlaw rep, Mr. Baynes. I guess you're not on the dodge anymore."

"Never was, Mr. Prime. In fact, I never yet figured out where all those rumors came from."

"From the way you braced that Cozart feller, I'd say you ain't no stranger to trouble. Didn't look like you got much backdown in your nature. Rumor has it your boys don't have none either."

"Facing trouble is one thing. Outlawing is something else. No Baynes rides outside the law. None ever has."

"Heard your son Milton run a sheriff plumb into the grave over in Texas."

"All right. I should have said no Baynes rides outside honest law."

Ruth asked, "Where are your sons now, Mr. Baynes?"

"Luke, the oldest, is a federal judge up in Wyoming. Milton, the next oldest, has a cattle ranch in Texas. Ward, the youngest, has a horse ranch in California about a day's ride east of Sacramento."

"And they're all married." Ruth made a sour mouth.

"Yes, ma'am. No matter, you'll be surrounded in Pioche by good-looking young miners."

"I'm not interested in miners. That's rotten, unhealthy work. They die too young."

"All right. We'll find you a nice young Mormon farmer. They're a healthy lot, and they bring produce for sale to Pioche."

"Oh, no you don't. I don't want to join a harem and have to argue with four or five other wives."

Darnell's hand rose again to rub his chin. "You're too hard to please, Miss Prime."

"Amen." Joshua Prime spat again at his favorite wheel and stared off into the distance, showing his daughter his own ability to ignore a hot glare.

She turned away from her father to smile at Darnell. "You'll get used to it."

"Used to what?"

"Shaving. You've been exploring your face all day. You look better, at least ten years younger. I knew you would."

Prime rolled his eyes skyward and lifted a hand, palm up, a gesture of helpless apology. "No offense, Mr. Baynes, but she's right. She don't mean no slight either. She's just a natural-born bothersome child."

She turned on the wagon seat to look up at Darnell. "How old are you?"

"Guess."

"Forty."

"Bad guess, but thank you. You're cold as winter. You know I have sons in their twenties."

"I bet you married young. Forty-five?"

"Warmer, but you're still cold."

"Forty-eight?"

"That's warmer, but I'm not answering any more. You owe me five or six questions now. They're adding up fast."

"Those weren't questions. They were guesses."

"They count."

"I should have known not to trust a man with a lawyer for a son."

"That's right. I admitted that up front. You had warning."

Darnell enjoyed Ruth's cheerful prying and easy laughter more with each passing day while they traveled at a pace comfortable for the horses. They passed through miserable weather and cutting wind on the way through Carson Pass, but nothing seemed to bother the durable

Primes. They shared a relaxed kinship more like congenial partners than a father and daughter.

Darnell came to envy the sturdy Joshua Prime, found himself wondering how much he might have missed by having no daughters of his own. He spent little time with that thought, quickly dismissing the idea when he recalled the hard life his sons had endured through the years. If he'd had a daughter, the poor child would have grown up tough as saddle leather without opportunity to develop any of the gentle female graces. Men taught sons manly conduct and responsibilities. Women taught daughters feminine skills, and Darnell had no woman. He didn't know how Prime managed. A daughter would have confounded Darnell after his wife died, growing up just when she needed a mother the most.

Then, one night after following the now downward-sloping trail for two days through the piñon-juniper foothills into the sage-covered flats, Darnell received a shock that set him back on his heels. He had walked a few steps away from the fire Prime always insisted on having and stood in the darkness. Since he always slept away from their campsite, Ruth must have assumed he'd departed for the night.

As Darnell stood in the darkness, staring up at the stars, Ruth's low voice came clearly through the quiet night. "Daddy."

"Yeah, honey?" Prime's answer came low but plain.

"Be careful with Mr. Baynes. He scares me."

"What?" Prime's voice raised in astonishment.

"He scares me, Daddy. He smiles and acts the perfect gentleman, but he's different. I've never been around anyone like him before. Daddy, Mr. Baynes doesn't really care about anything. He just doesn't give a damn."

"Don't cuss, Ruth. It ain't becoming."

"I know, Daddy. I'm sorry. But I think he's the most indifferent man I ever met. He covers it by seeming so good-natured, laughing and teasing, but do you remember how he handled that awful Stretch Cozart? Did you see his face? And I keep remembering his voice. I can't stop thinking about it. He didn't care what happened. Lots of men pretend not to care, but it's a big act. He really doesn't."

"He's a tough man, honey. I must have heard a hundred stories about him and his boys. Every one of those stories ends up with somebody or other getting killed or beat half to death."

"He must have a thousand enemies if half those stories are true, Daddy. All those people had friends and families. It's risky even to be around him."

"Well, honey, I'm not worried. Maybe it's been that way for him so long, he's used to it. Maybe that's why he don't seem to care. He'd be a nervous wreck for sure if he let it bother him."

"I think he's sad, Daddy, sad and lonely. He's

so nice and easy to talk to. But sometimes he just seems to drift away, like he's not even here but off somewhere else. I never saw a man so careful. He won't even camp with us, goes off and hides. He always knows where we are, but we never know where he sleeps. He never even comes back from the same direction he left."

Darnell turned away and silently sought his blankets, uneasy with himself, feeling vaguely ashamed for having overheard a private conversation, even by accident. He lay awake long into the night wondering why and how his name still carried so much worrisome burden. Even friendly people who were coming to like him couldn't shake off the weight of it. The empty legend of the marauding Baynes clan seemed to have a life of its own.

A sharp-eyed young woman, alerted by his name, looked closely and saw too much. She thought him to be sad and lonely. She'd probably be confused and even more uneasy if he tried to explain. He felt neither sadness nor loneliness. He felt empty, simply felt nothing at all, and she probably wouldn't understand how that was a very different thing indeed. He considered the situation with a detached sense of mild concern, wondering if any of this made any difference.

Of course it did. It made no sense to associate with people when his presence made them uncomfortable. He had come through the pass with them, thinking to be useful if the trip turned overly difficult. They'd need no help with the remainder of their travel. Now he'd ride on and relieve Ruth's mind.

She had decided that having him around brought danger. At least, he could ease that fear. A simple problem rightly had a simple solution. He'd shared a pleasant few days with them. Now it needed to be ended.

The next morning Darnell was already in the saddle when he approached their camp. He said, "I'll be riding on ahead now. It's been a pleasure." He leaned from the saddle, briefly gripped Prime's hand, tipped his hat to Ruth, and kicked his horse into a trot. Both of them stood with sleepy morning faces, caught in wordless surprise. He didn't look back.

FIVE

Eight days later, Darnell figured he should be drawing near to Hiko. If Pioche had the reputation of a wild mining town, Hiko's claim to fame came as a roost for outlaws, horse thieves, rustlers, and highwaymen.

Many Mormon farmers found themselves in trouble when driving their wagons toward home from Pioche. They ended up standing with hands in the air while money earned by selling their produce in Pioche went to highwaymen from Hiko. Darnell had heard that the Mormons developed clever hiding places in their wagons. The thieves countered by burning the wagons and sifting the ashes for gold or silver coins. The Mormons lost their sense of humor, started carrying guns, and showed they knew how to use them.

Cattlemen from Arizona and New Mexico lost herds when they ran into groups of heavily armed men who, sometimes with elaborate courtesy, offered them a chance to go home broke and without cattle but alive. Those cattle, it was rumored, grazed peacefully around Hiko and later brought top prices to feed Pioche miners. Evidently, if any kind of law existed in

Hiko, it recognized the outlaws as operating the major local industry and left them alone as long as they behaved inside the town limits. They must have honored the unspoken agreement pretty well; Hiko seldom had more than one or two killings a week.

Darnell rode past an isolated, abandoned homestead in the slanting light of late afternoon. On impulse, he turned back and slid from the saddle by the open doorway of the shack. He wandered through the windowless, doorless cabin, noting how boards had been ripped loose by travelers and fed to campfires. Well off any of the regular trails, the fire-darkened spots near the shack showed that it still attracted pilgrims. Gradually the forlorn little building was vanishing, piece by piece, just as the dreams of its builder must have crumbled.

The skeleton of the nearby barn leaned southward, its walls mostly stripped away, its roof still boasting a few shingles too high for passersby to knock down for burning without chancing a perilous climb. The old beam of its protruding hay lift pointed westward like the neck of a ghostly goose, probably indicating the direction its owner had headed if he survived the ruin of his hopes.

For the first time in years Darnell allowed his mind to range back to his abandoned land in Louisiana. Strange how this little place reminded him of his days in a loving home. His lips, cracked by the Nevada sun and wind, stretched into a painful smile at the absurdness of how this poor and dejected place should remind him of the spacious, solid buildings he'd proudly built in what seemed to be a prior life. This poor dry soil of gravel, sand, and sage couldn't compare to the rich Louisiana delta with its abundant rainfall. Yet, the comfortable home he'd abandoned had probably fallen apart just as this place had.

In one flash of time, one short day, he'd lost the woman he loved with all his heart, and his sons had lost their mother and their innocence. On the very day his boys lost their mother to a sudden fever, each of them had killed his first man. The six drunken fools who rode to his front doorstep that evening to draft his boys into the Confederate Army had pulled guns and fallen in seconds.

Darnell remembered standing in shocked silence, looking at the downed men, stunned with the realization of how well he'd trained his sons. He'd honestly had no glimmer of an idea until that moment that he'd reared young men so alert, so deadly, and so ready to follow his lead.

His own reaction had been an unthinking reflex when the drunken deputy sheriff lifted a gun. Six men died in about as many seconds because Darnell had trained his sons to have the same deadly response as his own. Instead of young horse trainers on a peaceful farm, they'd reacted like veteran soldiers, or if you listened to the false legend, like seasoned outlaws.

There had been no time for any command from him, not even a shout of warning. His sons had sent a hail of lead into that group of men before the mortally wounded deputy Darnell had shot could fall from his horse.

Within an hour, Darnell and his boys left an old way of life behind. Few reminders can be carried on horseback. The break had been clean if not painless. Somehow this forlorn little homestead brought back the memory and the ache. Spurred by a morbid curiosity he couldn't resist, he wandered in slow circles around the decaying building. He found no grave and felt so relieved his knees weakened under him. If this had been a home for a family and they left together, the dream could rise again in another place.

Darnell absently rubbed his pockets as if searching, suffering with the awareness that he had no memento of his wife, no picture, no lock of hair. The only thing he'd had, her wedding rings, he'd given to Ward on the eve of his engagement. Kit, Ward's lovely wife, now wore them, and she prized them. It was proper and fitting for family treasures to be passed down to the young. Darnell leaned his forehead against a weathered barn timber and drew a deep breath.

He couldn't remember her face anymore, that proud Spanish woman who had left an aristocratic family to give herself to a crude backwoods lad. Now he understood his own dismay. Now he knew why he felt empty, and the knowing hurt. She had slipped away. Foolishly, he'd felt her with him all these years, had taken her for granted, but some awful weakness in his mind had let her fade, and now she was gone.

He allowed his hands to continue their idiotic search of his pockets, searching for something — a ribbon, a button, anything. But nothing remained. She had slipped away, leaving nothing for him to hold.

He wouldn't camp here. Something about being here brought old hurts to the surface. Besides, the old fire sites plainly told of frequent visitors, and he wanted no company. Back in the saddle, he rode less than a hundred yards to the steep edge of an arroyo, walked his mount along the top until he found a gentler slope, and slid to the bottom. If travelers stopped at the old shack, they'd never even see him.

Forcing his mind blank, he stripped off the saddle and pack, hobbled his horses, and fed them each a quart of grain and a generous drink from the big canteens the pack horse carried. Darkness fell quickly when the sun fell behind the mountains, and Darnell rolled into his blankets to avoid the gathering chill. He didn't bother trying to eat anything. He felt neither hunger nor thirst. Wanting to drift quickly into sleep, he felt a touch of anger while watching the stars with wide eyes. The hardest thing for a man to do is wish himself to doze. Sleep comes or it doesn't, but wishing for it almost guarantees a restless wait.

The wind died, leaving a quiet so dense it probably would have wakened him anyway. No kangaroo rat came snooping. No chipmunk scurried. No bird twittered. Darnell began to feel spooked, pulled his boots on, and with one of his blankets across his shoulders, climbed to the edge of the arroyo. He closed his eyes in the inky darkness and slowly swung his head back and forth, concentrating, listening as hard as he could. Sure enough, he heard something, soft and distant. He made his best guess and decided it was horses, traveling slow.

He eased back down the slope, strapped on his Navy, and picked up his Spencer. With the speed of long practice, he saddled his mount and tied the pack on the other animal. When a man feels uneasy, the fool inside says to ignore it, sneers about the child afraid of the dark, but the wise man listens to inner whispers of danger and rebuffs the inner fool. Foolhardy actions can be costly, but cautious moves never cost much. The wisest and most dangerous fighting men in the history of the world always planned and prepared to retreat in good order if faced with an ill-behaved turn of fortune.

The sudden impulse to smile stiffened Darnell's mouth and he almost split a cracked lip. A trick of memory brought back the time the irrepressible, smirking Milt came stalking into camp holding a bloody knife. Two Comanche warriors had tried to slip up and steal their horses. Milt killed them both so silently the rest of the family never heard a thing.

Milt, waving the knife gently in front of him, said, "I tell you, Pa, surprising somebody who's trying to surprise me is like sparking a pretty woman. It warms me all around my private parts." Of all his trail-hardened family with their long experience in woodland crafts, Darnell knew Milt had the most intensely honed instincts, came closest to the perfection of an invincible predator. The Comanche warriors, with the confidence of their courage and skill, had not recognized their bad turn of fortune until too late.

Darnell stood with a hand on the muzzle of each of his horses. He didn't need a greeting from them to alert night riders of his presence. The click of a hoof on a stone snapped Darnell's head to the left. His guess had been accurate. Now the low shuffle of hooves on the sandy soil told him more than one animal moved closer.

A man spoke in a low tone, but the surrounding quiet let Darnell hear him as if he rode at the man's shoulder. "There it is. I told you I could find it."

Another answered. "I'm still not sure we're doing the right thing. I think we ought to take him to town and let the law handle him."

The first voice came loud and rough. "Stop your whining. I swear, Nolan, I think you squat to pee. The law won't do a thing but turn him loose. The law is probably his partner. The law would probably lock you up for bothering this horse thief." The man came down hard on "the law" every time he spoke the words, using them with such sneering contempt they sounded like curses. "The closest real law is clear back in Utah. You want to take him home with you?"

When no response came, the hard voice spoke again. "That old barn still has a hay lift beam. Best substitute for a tree we got for miles around here. When I found this place there were fire marks all around it. I bet leaving him hanging here will give a good lesson to half the horse thieves in Nevada."

"It still isn't right, Asa. None of the others wanted anything to do with it either. I only came along because I thought you'd cool down, and I could talk sense to you."

Saddles creaked and Darnell heard boots land on the hard ground. "You get him down off that horse, Nolan. I'm going to start a fire."

"Why do you need a fire?"

"I want to see him die, that's why. I want to be sure." The crack of a boot against wood came several times, followed by the squeak of pulling nails.

Darnell felt sure his horses would keep quiet now, so he walked closer. He moved slowly, edging forward, confident the riders wouldn't detect him. The moonless night wasn't all that dark with the heavens sprinkled with stars, but these men were too busy with their own affairs to pay attention. In moments, Darnell expected them to be blinded by their own fire.

The blaze of a match proved him right. In seconds, dry wood seemed almost to explode into flame. The flickering light outlined three men. One, hatless, had slumped to the ground. One of the men kicked the slumped figure and pointed to the hay lift, a black line against the stars.

"You see that, horse thief? That's your tree. You're going to hang there and ripen in the sun. You're our lesson to all your kind." He kicked the slumped figure again.

The other man stepped between them. "That's enough, Asa. You been hitting this man ever since we tied him up. Hit him again and we're going to tangle. You hear me?"

Asa snickered. "Don't get your knickers in a knot, Nolan. I already hit him enough to tire of just doing that. I'm going to hang him now." He stalked to his horse and came back with a rope. He tossed the rope over the hay lift and turned toward the others. "Drag him over here and stand him up."

"Aren't you going to put him back on his horse?"

"Naw. I'm just going to hoist him up so we can watch him dance awhile."

"You'll do it by yourself then. I'm not for this."

Asa stalked over to the seated figure, flipped the loop over his head, and walked back to stand under the hay lift. He grabbed the rope hanging across the beam and jerked. The seated figure fell over and slid forward. Asa took another grip higher on the rope and lifted his feet off the ground, putting his full weight on the rope. The prone figure slid toward him another few inches. "Come on, you heavy son of a bitch. Come on." The man on the ground gagged and coughed.

"Asa, for God's sake. I never saw such meanness." Nolan stepped forward and pulled back against the rope.

Darnell dropped to one knee and cranked a shell into his Spencer. Both the standing figures spun to face the darkness. Asa's hands dropped away from the rope, and he pulled a pistol from his belt.

"Get on your horses and ride away."

Nolan walked toward Darnell's voice and lifted a hand to shield his eyes. "Who's out there?"

"Never mind. Get mounted. You're leaving."

"This feller's a horse thief. We brought him here to hang him."

"You changed your mind. Ride while you can. I'm tired of waiting. You can leave that pistol behind, just so it doesn't get you into trouble."

Asa stood facing Darnell, but his searching moves with the pistol and his head left no doubt he couldn't find the voice from the darkness.

Nolan turned toward the horses and said, "Drop that damn gun, and let's get out of here."

"This here pistol cost me twenty-five dollars."

"Buy candy next time. It'll sweeten your nature." Nolan sounded pleased to be leaving.

Darnell pointed his Spencer, holding low. Without enough light to see his sights, he could only point the rifle like a shotgun and hold low, knowing most night shots miss from going too high. "It's getting late and I'm tired. I'll count to myself. When I get to three, I'm going to kill you, Asa, unless that pistol's on the ground and your butt's in the saddle."

Nolan reached his horse and mounted. "For God's sake, Asa, come on. You can't fight a man you can't see."

Asa pulled his pistol around in front of him. With his back to the fire, the weapon disappeared in shadow. "I dropped it. I'm leaving."

Darnell squeezed off a shot. A puff of sand erupted in front of Asa, and he jerked so hard his hat fell off. He crouched, both hands gripping his thigh. "You shot me. The bullet glanced up and got me."

"Pull that gun out of your pants and throw it down. I'll count to three again."

Asa pulled the gun and pitched it down next to the fire, careful that the weapon landed in good light. "I'm bleeding."

"Did I forget to tell you I'd shoot after counting three if you're not in the saddle?"

Asa hopped to his horse and climbed aboard. His movements showed he'd been nicked but hadn't been severely wounded. "We'll be back, damn you. We'll be back. You'll be sorry." He kicked his horse into a gallop. Nolan followed at a more cautious pace. The darkness swallowed them in seconds.

Darnell waited until the sound of the departing horses died, and the eerie silence returned. The man by the fire came to his feet, the rope still trailing from his neck across the hay lift. "I'm mighty obliged, mister. You sure enough saved my life." He spoke without lifting his voice.

Darnell, still listening, didn't answer.

"Are you going to show yourself, mister? Or am I talking to a ghost out there in the dark?"

"Walk away from the fire. Just come out here toward my voice."

The man turned away from the barn and stumbled backward on unsteady legs, pulling the rope a few inches at a time over the hay lift beam until it fell to the ground. Then he turned and walked with his upper body twisted sideways to keep the pressure of the trailing rope off his throat. After a few steps, he stumbled and dropped to one knee. He took several deep breaths and struggled again to his feet.

Darnell watched his wobbly progress and noted that, while the poor devil might be having a hard time of it, his sense of direction was perfect. He walked toward the voice in the darkness with the accuracy of a dog on scent, even though his weak legs sent him tottering in an irregular line.

"They whip up on you pretty good, boy?"

"Yes, sir, they did that. They surely did. Mostly that fellow Asa. I thought he'd never get tired of it."

"Horse thieves don't bring out the best in folks."

"No, sir. Guilty or not."

Darnell backed up to the edge of the arroyo and eased down the slope a few steps so he could outline his man against the sky and the fire behind him. "You're doing fine." Figuring that his man's eyes hadn't had time to adjust from the firelight, he added, "A few steps more and you'll come to the edge of a steep slope. Be careful."

"Yes, sir. I will, and I thank you again." The unsteady steps shortened and started to slide along the ground as he felt his way. Even so, when he came to the edge, his legs buckled. He fell on his face and slid several feet. When he tried to rise, his legs gave way again and he rolled the rest of the way. He lay still for several seconds, breathing heavily. When his breath steadied, he chuckled. "Next time you say something about a steep slope, I promise to pay more attention. Yes, sir, you mean what you say."

"You just sit right where you are. Don't move. I'm going to look around."

Another chuckle. "I'll do that most gladly, sir. I'm not anxious to be running around much right now, and that's a fact."

Darnell made a cautious circuit about a hundred yards around where he'd left his horses. If Asa planned to bring friends like he'd promised, they hadn't arrived yet, nor had Asa circled back. He moved quickly to the fire and scattered it. No need to leave a beacon to guide them if they were coming. He grabbed the reins of the remaining horse and eased back to the arroyo.

The man he'd saved from a rope lay in the darkness exactly where Darnell had left him. Without comment, Darnell pulled his blade and cut the rope off the man's neck. Another slash and the man's hands were freed. As soon as the ropes fell from him, the man sat up and started rubbing his hands. "I think they'll be all right after a while."

"What's that?"

"My hands. I'm getting some feeling back already. That Asa tied me so tight my hands turned to dead sticks."

"Sorry. I didn't know. I could have cut you loose before I scouted around."

He chuckled. "I don't think so. No call for you to cut loose a horse thief and then leave him alone with your horses."

Darnell stiffened his mouth to protect his cracked lips from his temptation to grin. "How did you fall so low, young man? Stealing horses isn't a smart thing to be doing."

"I didn't, sir. I heard they were paying gun wages in Pioche, so I headed that way. This fellow was having a hard time with a big bunch of horses and asked me to help. I hired on not knowing those broom tails were stolen. When those men came up on us, I was caught like a dumb sage hen. He rode off on his fastest horse and left me to twist in the wind." He rubbed his hands for a moment in silence before adding quietly, "I might like to trouble him about that, if I ever cross his trail again. Yes, sir, that would pleasure me, now that my hands feel like they might work right again someday."

"You heard people wanted hired guns in Pioche?"

'Yes, sir. Heard the mine owners are hiring more guards. Word out is that there's a big tussle about to happen."

"You a hired gun?"

"I guess not. Since those boys took mine away from me, I don't even have one anymore. Last thing I wanted to do anyhow, but it'd be a job. A hungry man needs to work."

"You hungry?"

"A manner of speaking, sir. I'm broke. But if you have any water, I'd be grateful for a turn at it."

"Sorry." Darnell handed one of his canteens to the man. "I wasn't thinking. I've grown used to riding alone. And speaking of riding, let's move away from here. Those fellows might come back like they promised. Can you ride?"

Without answering, the man rose and moved toward his horse. He stood beside the animal for a few moments, taking deep breaths. Then he swung into the saddle.

Darnell led the way southward for about two hours. The moon rose as they rode, sailing fat and bright into a clear sky. Finally, he came to an old buffalo wallow, a depression deep enough to hide the horses well enough until morning. He slid from the saddle. "We'll bide here awhile, if you're agreeable."

"We haven't gone far, sir. Won't be a problem for them if they take a notion to trail us."

"Last night I figure I gave fair warning. If they want to shed more blood, they're free men."

The young fellow dropped to the ground. The ride through the cold night air must have been good for him. His legs showed more strength, but he was quick to find a place to sit down. "Best we not unsaddle, don't you think, sir?"

"Didn't plan to."

"I brought the hanging rope with me. I think I got a broken rib or two. Once I heard if a man wrapped a rope around and around the sore place it made breathing hurt less. Would you help me try that, sir?"

"Sure." Darnell helped the man out of his shirt and wound the rope around the slim frame. The young fellow set his jaw and held his breath as the strands tightened around his body, but he made no sound.

When Darnell tied the end, his only clue that the process had caused pain came from a whistling breath as fast as that of a running man. Horse thief or not, he was a proud youngster, showing a broad streak of toughness.

"I have some buffalo chips on that pack horse. We can make a little fire here in this wallow. I don't think anybody could have followed us close enough to see it, and it won't burn long. You'd be needing a cup of coffee, and I can fry some sow belly. Like I said, I've grown to riding alone, so my manners have suffered."

"That so? Surprise for me. I never pictured you traveling alone without your boys, Mr. Baynes."

Darnell's stomach muscles tightened. "I never told you my name, young man."

"No, sir, you don't need to. I didn't know you at first from just your voice, but when I saw how big you are, I knew you right off. You got an easy way of moving around that's easy to remember."

"Do I know you? Who are you, son?"

"I'm Fane Trampe, Mr. Baynes."

Darnell, crouched beside the man, came to his feet. The rising moon now lighted the sage-littered plain with a brilliant glow. His gaze had been roving, just to be sure the hanging party didn't turn the tables and slip up on him. For a moment, he forgot them. He focused his attention on the battered face of the hatless man seated in front of him. He couldn't be sure what this young fellow might look like in normal times. The features were too swollen and the light too weak.

Darnell took a step back. Either this polite young man had taken another's name or a deadly enemy of his family had risen from the dead.

SIX

"Fane, I thought you were dead."

"Yes, sir, I know. I guess I'm the only man ever to face Ward Baynes when he had a mad on and live to tell it. He looked down his gun barrel at me in that doctor's house, and I was too weak to move a finger. Ward just decided not to kill me. I thought I dreamed it, couldn't believe it, but the doctor said it was so. Tell me the truth. Did Ward ever do that before?"

"No, I don't think so, but he said the doctor told him you were dying, wouldn't live till morning."

"I know. No offense, Mr. Baynes, but I never thought your boy Ward was the kind to be turned away by any kind of talk. When he's on the warpath, Ward has hard ways."

"Most anybody would be sore, seems to me. All you Trampes did was shoot his hired hand in both legs, run off with Ward's maid and his son, and promise to kill them unless you got paid off."

One hand pressed against his side, Trampe eased himself gently to the ground. A slow expulsion of breath hinted that the move from the sitting position to lie on his side gave him relief.

"I'll not dodge blame, Mr. Baynes. That was a low thing to do, and I was there, but it wasn't my idea, and that's the straight truth. My pa did that on a sudden notion, and he came to be sorry after he had time to ponder what he'd done."

"My oldest, Luke, said from the start that the whole thing didn't sound like you, Fane."

Trampe lowered his head and spoke so softly Darnell leaned forward to hear. "That Luke, now there's a real man. We'd have been friends, me and Luke, if things had been different."

Darnell matched Trampe's soft voice. "I thought you'd like to know Luke spoke up for you. Ward listened to Luke, Fane, and he didn't answer back. That's how Ward does when he agrees. Hell, we all listen to Luke."

Darnell dropped his hat to the ground and cupped his hands behind his ears. Trampe stiffened in alarm and lay perfectly still while Darnell listened to the night. He relaxed when Darnell replaced his hat and spoke again. "Ward said you asked him to look after Arlo when he had you under the gun. Since he thought you were dying, he decided you deserved to go in peace. Ward appreciated your asking help for your brother with what he thought might be your last breath. He sets store by men who stand with family. Did you know he took your brother home with him? Arlo lives with Ward and his wife now."

"I rode by there and took a look. I saw Arlo

dancing. You know Arlo dances when he's real happy?"

Darnell chuckled. "No, I never saw him do that."

"He's simple, but he knows people would laugh at him if they saw him do it. He's careful. He doesn't really dance. It's just kind of a bouncing around and singing to himself when he's feeling good about everything. I remember my pa used to say Arlo lives close to the angels. I guess that's the way with some simple-minded people. Maybe all of them aren't that way, but I think Pa was right about Arlo."

"Fane, did you ride onto Ward's property?" Darnell didn't bother to keep doubt from his voice.

"Yes, sir. Most careful riding I ever did, and I kept a safe distance. Used a telescope I had at the time. Ward would kill me on sight. I wouldn't have a chance, quick as he is."

"I guess you didn't talk to Arlo?"

"I didn't dare try, Mr. Baynes. Once I saw how happy he was, I rode on. He has a home now. That's more than I can say. Best for him I don't upset his good luck."

Darnell realized he'd not yet started the fire, so he gathered the makings from the canvas bag he carried on his pack horse when crossing desert country, started the tiny blaze, and poured water from a canteen into the coffee-pot.

Fane spoke in a low tone. "As for me, a little

coffee would go good. Don't do any cooking for me. I'm too tuckered out to eat."

"All right." Darnell turned quickly away from the fire so his eyes would adjust again to the night.

"That Dr. Stone was a friend to me, Mr. Baynes. He gave me money when I got well enough to ride. Said Ward gave it to him so I would be buried decent and proper. Did he do that?"

"Yes, he did, Fane. I know because Ward didn't have money with him. Had to ask me for it."

"Well, fancy that." Trampe's voice trailed away, and one hand cautiously rose to explore his bruised face. After a long pause, he said, "You might tell him the money kept me from going hungry. It took me a while to get well enough to work. Tell him I'm obliged."

"I'll tell him."

"You don't think he'll be mad at Dr. Stone, will he?"

"No."

"I wouldn't want to be the cause of making Ward mad at anybody."

"I understand." Darnell put a hand over his mouth. He made himself say no more, even though fury raged through him like a flash of fever. He had long ago lost patience with those who held to the common belief that his youngest son was a ferocious, inhuman killer.

"I think I'll go ahead and get some sleep. I'm

mighty beat down. Save my coffee for tomorrow, will you?"

"Sure."

"Only one more thing, Mr. Baynes."

"What's that, Fane?"

"You ought to know I swore a solemn oath. I swore to God I'd never lift a gun against a Baynes again. When I saw Arlo so happy, it buckled something in me. His clothes were new and clean and everything. I asked Ward to look after Arlo because I thought I was finished. I heard the shooting outside the doctor's house where I was laid up, so I figured you got Pa. Nobody was left to look after Arlo. Jole went after that Mexican maid of Ward's, so Pa hung him on a tree and beat him with a wet rope till he was near dead. Then Pa ran him off. Nobody was left in my family. Did you know that?"

"Maria told us about your pa whipping Jole and running him off, so we knew about that. Terrible thing. Even after being insulted and knocked around, she said she felt sorry for Jole."

"Pa nearly went wild over that. We never came to much, Mr. Baynes, but Pa tried to teach us not to act offensive to women."

Darnell thought for a long time before he spoke again. Trampe deserved to know, but telling him might be a ghastly mistake. "You still awake?"

"Yes, sir."

"Fane, Milt ran Jole down and killed him."

Trampe took a long, deep breath and expelled

it slowly through pursed lips. "Mr. Baynes, that's a heavy load off my mind."

"I don't know what that means, Fane."

"Me and Pa figured somebody would hang Jole someday. He was my brother, but he was lowdown. At least Milt kills clean. Nobody wants a brother, no matter how bad he is, to die on a rope. There was a time when I thought I'd have to kill Jole myself."

"Why do you say that, Fane? That'd be a terrible thing. What caused you to have such an awful idea?"

"To keep Pa from it. Pa would have died from doing it, but he was getting closer and closer. I could see it coming. If I hadn't talked Pa into running him off, I think he might have done it over Jole going after that woman we took from Ward's house when we took his boy. He came near to beating Jole to death with that rope. Pa wasn't all that much of a good man. I know that. But he had his righteous side."

"I'll testify to that."

"Fills a man with wonder, doesn't it?"

"What?"

"I had one brother lift a gun against your family in Louisiana. One of you killed him. Pa figured to get revenge when none was due him. So we carried off Ward's baby boy, and you came after us. You killed another brother and my pa and wounded me bad, but Ward let me off and took Arlo home to look after him. Arlo looks mighty happy living with Ward Baynes, a man thought to have no soft feelings. Seeing Arlo being looked after so kindly tore me up. I swore not to lift a gun against you Baynes men again, and look what happened. You saved my life today. Do you suppose the Almighty decided to let me live because I took that oath? Wouldn't that be a wonder?"

Darnell recognized the tremor in Trampe's voice and quickly shook out his blankets to cover him. The proud young fool planned to lie there shivering in the cold desert night rather than ask for anything, and Darnell had been too caught up in the strange conversation to offer. Trampe probably didn't want to face bending to remove his own boots either, so Darnell pulled them off for him, not answering the repeated mutters of thanks from the exhausted young man.

Wide-awake and shaking inside, Darnell poured himself a cup of coffee and stomped the glow from the last embers. He pulled his sheepskin coat from the pack and shrugged into it, prepared to watch through till morning.

The stillness of a high desert night, stars closer and more neighborly than anywhere else on earth, made it easier for a man filled with wonder to think about a power greater than himself. The cruel sadness that struck him at the pitiful abandoned homestead came back to mind. Even in its grip, he'd noticed no resemblance to anything that ought to remind him of his lost home. How strange that echoes from years ago and miles away came to haunt him at such a remote and unlikely spot.

A Trampe had been one of the fools who died a few feet from his doorstep that awful evening back in 1863, causing him to take his family away from Louisiana forever, causing the rise of endless false rumors branding the Baynes clan as outlaws. Then, years later, Trampes had attacked Ward's household and carried off one of his trusted servants along with his son. That incident ended up with Baynes men killing two more Trampes. Now all that remained of that family were weak-minded Arlo and Fane. Had he known that deadly rope circled Fane Trampe's neck tonight, he would never have lifted a hand.

After all the dying in a vicious, senseless blood feud, how could it be possible that the only remaining Trampe other than the harmless and gentle Arlo would be rescued by a Baynes? To call such an accident anything other than a miracle would be ridiculous. If it hadn't been a dark night, Darnell knew he would have recognized Fane. In that case, he would have watched the hanging with grim satisfaction, even vindictive amusement. A man might stir himself to save a complete stranger, simply because the thought of hanging a human being sickened him, but it would be outrageous nonsense to rescue a blood enemy. A saint might do it, but not Darnell Baynes.

He idly ran a finger across his cracked lips,

feeling the rough edges of the peeling skin. Slowly he changed his position, shifting his body to scan another section of the moonlit desert. His mind could move down twisted and tortured corridors, but his eyes and ears would still signal anything of interest to a hunted man.

Nothing moved except the leaves of the scraggly, scattered sage, trembling silently in a vagrant breeze that touched first here and then yonder. Plains Indians used the fragrant plant in their purification rites. Darnell always thought the smell of sage the cleanest perfume in creation.

Whether a man approached the Almighty or pagan spirits for guidance, it made sense to come to the conference as clean and neat as he could manage. A man should show as much courtesy as he could muster when he came asking favors. On impulse, he came to his feet and moved silently up the edge of the wallow. He stripped a handful of leaves from the nearest sage bush and backed down the slope. After standing for a few moments without moving, listening to the night, he crushed the leaves between his palms and rubbed the shreds across his face and the front of his coat.

Darnell moved his lips when he spoke, but no sound came as he stood with his eyes raised to the stars. "Why did you bring me here and get me into this? What do you want me to do with this boy? I'm going to sit here all night trying to think all this out and make sense of it. I know you don't favor doing my work for me, but I'd be obliged if you'd give me a nudge, just a little hint."

He brushed the bits of sage off his hands and the front of his coat. Then he stood for a while with his fragrant hands cupped to his face before he lifted the Spencer to cradle it across his chest. A comfortable place to sit, quiet walks around the camp from time to time to avoid getting stiff, a fight against sleep in the wee hours, and a lot of thinking lay ahead. Dawn would be slow coming.

SEVEN

The little pronghorn dropped in his tracks. His companions scattered and vanished with magical speed, covering ground with great bounds to disappear behind folds in a desert that fooled the eye by pretending to be flat. Darnell turned from the downed animal to watch Trampe jerk awake and struggle to a sitting position, eyes wide with panic.

"Good morning, sleepyhead."

"What you shooting at? They coming up on us?"

"I just shot fresh meat. We'll eat good today."

Trampe reached for a boot. "Is that a good idea, Mr. Baynes? They might hear the shot and come a-running if they're nearby."

"Think back. Didn't I tell you if they come after us the blood will be on their heads?"

"Yes, sir, but I never got around to telling you. You only saw two, but there were six of them. The other four didn't fancy riding around in the night to hang me. They felt this morning would be soon enough."

"If they trouble me, Fane, they'll ride home across saddles." Darnell came to his feet, reloaded, and walked to the pronghorn that had wandered close to the camp in the early morning. With the skill of long experience aided by a carefully honed skinning knife, he gutted the little animal, removed the hide, and wrapped the choice pieces in it. In less than fifteen minutes, he dropped the meat and sank to one knee to put a match to the fire he'd laid in the night. "I hope you're hungry. We have no time to dry this meat, so we'll have to eat as much as we can before it sours. Let your belt out a notch and get ready to do your part. The more we swallow, the less we'll have to carry."

"You plan to let me ride with you for a while, Mr. Baynes?"

"If you take to the idea."

"I'd be obliged." Trampe pulled on his second boot and came to his feet. He straightened with elaborate caution, one hand pressing his side. "Feast today, famine tomorrow, as my pa used to say. That's why belts have more than one hole punched in them."

"Feel any better?"

"Hurts worse all over, but I feel rested. You should have woke me up, Mr. Baynes. I could have stood watch."

Darnell looked at the swollen bruises distorting Trampe's face. "Asa bust any knuckles?"

"I hope so. He sure took to pounding me after they tied my hands. It's a mystery how men take a liking for different things. I never could find any pleasure in hitting a man who's tied up. Asa was the only one. Those other boys didn't seem to agree with it, but nobody stopped him."

"Each man seeks his own kind of comfort. Speaking of comfort reminds me." Darnell walked to his mount and dug into a saddlebag. "I think you'll feel better with this near to hand." He handed Trampe his spare Navy, belt, and holster. "Seems to me your custom is to go armed, and I notice those fellows forgot to return your irons last night in their rush to join their friends."

Trampe stood shifting the weapon from one hand to the other as if it burned his fingers.

"Strap it on, Fane. It'll free your hands to eat." Darnell knelt to turn the strips of meat in the skillet.

"Mr. Baynes, this here Navy Colt costs more than twenty dollars. I got no money at all."

"Gift."

Trampe swung the belt around his hips and buckled it. He started to pull the weapon from the holster but stopped and lifted a questioning glance to Darnell.

"Go on. Get the feel of it."

"No offense, Mr. Baynes, but I'm stumped. I can't figure a Baynes handing me a gun. I'm scared to touch it. You know as well as I do . . ." He stopped and looked away.

"Go ahead. Speak your piece."

"Every time a Trampe touches a gun around a Baynes he dies."

"You said you wouldn't lift a gun against me. I take your word."

Trampe, moving slowly, turned away and slid the Navy from its holster. He hoisted the weapon, testing the weight and feel, looked down the barrel, examined the loads, and returned it to the holster. Throughout the whole procedure the weapon pointed well away from Darnell. "It's loaded."

"A man might as well carry a holster full of rocks as an unloaded gun. Go ahead and try a few shots. Shoots true for me, but guns are notional. Sometimes they shoot different for one man than they do for another."

"You don't care about the noise bringing those fellows down on us, Mr. Baynes?"

"Thought we already talked about that."

"Yes, sir." Trampe scanned the surrounding desert before he turned a troubled face to Darnell. "You know, they didn't see you. Riding with me puts you under the gun too if they catch us."

Darnell scraped strips of meat onto a tin plate and shoved it toward Trampe, a fork resting along the edge. "Take big bites. I don't have an extra knife for you. I'll eat from the skillet. More where that came from, Fane. If they trail us, they'll see we rode from that old homestead together and camped together. That's as good as seeing us with our arms around each other, don't you think?"

He added more meat to the skillet, spearing browned strips with his knife and allowing them to cool briefly before nibbling at them. For every strip taken from the frying pan he added another, cooking more while he ate what he deemed ready.

Trampe ate in silence, accepting more when Darnell occasionally hoisted the skillet and extended it toward him. Finally, still chewing, he mumbled, "Don't seem proper to return a favor by calling down trouble on your head. I really figure those boys will trail us, Mr. Baynes. They're likely to start shooting if they catch us."

"Catch us, you say? You keep talking about them catching us. Young man, for anybody to catch us, we've got to be running. I don't feel like running. If those fellows want to find trouble, we're here. No cause for us to make life hard for them. You got to take a more neighborly attitude, Fane. Show a more generous disposition. That's the way to make friends."

Trampe chuckled and then flinched. He closed his eyes for a moment. "Don't make me laugh, Mr. Baynes. It hurts a man with a mashed face and busted ribs."

The meager fire died under the frying pan. Unconcerned, Darnell continued to eat the half-cooked meat until the pan sat empty. "Been awhile since we took a look around. I'll clean up and tighten the cinches and get ready to ride. You go see if your friends are rushing up here to die this morning."

The utensils packed and the horses ready to go, Darnell turned to summon Trampe. At that moment, Trampe called, "I think I see riders."

"We'll meet them right here. Wouldn't be sociable to make them ride any farther than they have to." Darnell walked up beside Trampe. "First time in years I've ridden with anybody but my own boys, Fane. Hope you don't mind if I sort of make suggestions about how to handle this."

"No, sir, I don't mind. In fact, I'm mighty curious about what you have in mind."

"Good. We already have the horses in a good place. We shouldn't have to worry about them getting hit by gunfire where they are. I hate when one of my horses gets shot. Aggravates me to see an animal suffer. Besides, it can be inconvenient."

Muscles working in his jaw, Trampe kept his gaze locked in the direction of the approaching riders. He made no comment, but he remained perfectly motionless to show he was paying attention.

"As soon as they get close enough to see us nice and plain, we'll step out of this wallow. We want them to see us standing out in the open. We want no mistake about what we're doing. We're waiting for them to come up. Not hiding. Not running. Waiting. Got it?"

"Yes, sir." Trampe's voice came strong and clear, no nervous strain or tremble in the man's tone.

Darnell nodded in satisfaction. "I take them for dumb farm boys. I don't expect them to stand off and plink at us. If they do what we want, they'll ride right up close. We'll stand on the very edge of this wallow. If shooting starts, one step back puts us sliding down the slope. We'll be low game, sliding and half-hidden, making hard targets for them. Can you shoot while moving, Fane?"

"I'm right good with a handgun, Mr. Baynes." His response came in the flat monotone of a mildly insulted man.

"That's the spirit. Don't wait for them to get close before you draw. Reach down and draw real slow and obvious. You might make a show of checking your loads. Then stand there with gun in hand. I'll be holding my Spencer in plain sight after making sure they see me cock it. We want them to feel like they're riding up to men eager to smell gun smoke. Farm boys get fidgets and loose bowels when they run into that kind of attitude from folks they expect to run."

"All right." Trampe's voice came low, the routine tone of a man receiving instructions for a serene day's work.

Darnell climbed the slope and stood tall and straight. When Trampe joined him and moved a few feet away, Darnell spoke again. "I haven't had this much fun since I watched the hogs eat my little brother."

Trampe snickered. "I haven't heard that one since I was a little kid. It already had a beard down to its knees way back then. That old Louisiana joke makes me homesick."

As the riders drew closer Darnell put on a big

smile. "Start grinning real big, Fane, sort of get your face warmed up for looking like a kid wearing his best clothes in a mud hole." Darnell turned his head as if speaking to someone behind him and said, "Don't think I'm going off my top when I talk to men back in that wallow when nobody's there. They don't know that."

"Mr. Baynes, if I were one of them right now, riding toward you, I'd point my horse's nose another direction and strap on my best hurry-up spurs. You're having a big frolic, but I'm getting a knot in my middle. I swear, they're coming right to us like you were pulling them in with a rope."

"What did they take off you, Fane? Rifle and pistol?"

"And my skinning knife."

"That all?"

"Yes, sir." Trampe's voice took on an edge. "Ain't that enough? I was like a setting hen on a clutch of eggs. I just sat there with my mouth open when they rode up and threw down on me. I sure enough wasn't expecting anything like that."

"Now, now, don't get randy. Big smile. Look like they're bringing you candy. Hear that? Can you do rhymes too, Fane?"

Smiling broadly, Trampe said, "Mr. Baynes, I can feel my hair turning white, but I'm standing here giggling like an idiot. Don't talk to me any more. I never saw a man like you in my life."

The four horsemen, rifles cradled across chests, didn't rein in until they were only about twenty feet away. As soon as they halted, Darnell called, "Howdy, boys! Glad to see you. I won the bet. My son here got tired of waiting for you. He bet me you were going to let us down and not come at all."

"We come after that horse thief standing there grinning, but we're glad to catch both of you." The minute he spoke Darnell recognized Asa. Moments later, his horse shifted so the bandage on his thigh came into view.

"Yep, you caught us. Sure did. Now you boys just drop the stuff right where you are and ride on about your business. We thank you for going to all the trouble."

The oldest of the four, a man probably in his mid-twenties, leaned forward and turned his head slightly, as if to hear better. "Drop what stuff? What're you talking about?"

"I told my son you'd return everything. He described you fellows, and I told him you didn't sound like people who wouldn't return borrowed tools."

"Borrowed tools?" The man sat back in the saddle as if pushed back by astonishment. "Borrowed tools?"

"Yep. My son said you borrowed his rifle, pistol, and knife. Just drop them right where you are, and you can be on your way with a clear conscience. You did the right thing, bringing them back. Shows you're men of good character."

"Your son?" The man couldn't seem to catch up with the conversation.

"Adopted him, just last night. He's a good boy."

"Never mind all this palaver." Asa shifted the rifle across his chest. "We come to hang him, you fool, and maybe you too. Looks like you're in with him."

Holding his wide smile, Darnell spoke without shifting his eyes from the mounted men. "George, if I get distracted, shoot that one first, the one with his laundry on his leg."

Trampe chimed in. "I want Asa. He's special to me. I got him at the top of my dance card."

Darnell chuckled in pretended impatience. "All right, Fane, all right, first come, first served. No need to get in a fuss with your brother."

Asa's eyes darted frantically left and right, scanning the edge of the wallow. The other men tightened reins, causing their horses to edge away a few steps. Only Asa seemed excited. Darnell figured the others to be calmer men, probably happy to get their horses back and unenthused about burning powder to prove how brave they were.

Darnell took a step forward. "If you forgot to bring my son's tools, Asa, just drop your own right where you are, and we'll take them in trade. We won't trouble you to ride all that way back for Fane's gear, and we're in a little bit of a hurry anyhow. We got business down south."

Asa spat between his teeth and sneered. "Crazy bastard."

A rugged, square-shouldered young rider

with a torn shirt grinned and said, "I don't think so, Asa. I got business up north." He cautiously reined his horse around.

"So long, Nolan. Long life."

Nolan stopped his horse and looked back when he heard Darnell speak his name. "You know me?"

"Met you in the dark, but I like to tally young men with enough sense to have a future. So long, Nolan. Tell your folks you met Darnell Baynes while passing through Nevada."

The other two men's heads jerked and their eyes widened, sparse movements, but clear signals of surprise. Darnell's grin widened at the predictable response to his name. Both of them, as one, started to turn their horses. One said over his shoulder, "I'm Tom Ott, and this is my brother Danien, Baynes. Nice meeting you. We'll be going now. Got work to do."

Darnell dropped his easygoing tone. "Stop right there!" Asa stopped his mount, already half-turned. His three companions reined to a halt. "Not you boys, Nolan. You and the Otts go on about your business. Asa's the one not finished here." Darnell had narrowed his attention to the cocked rifle across Asa's chest, but he could still see the other three men ease their mounts back into motion, moving away.

Asa's face had gone dead white. The hand holding his reins trembled like an aspen leaf, and the other showed white at the trigger guard of his rifle. He licked lips gone dry. "I'll be going on with my friends. I guess they decided to let you off this time."

"Drop the rifle."

"I ain't giving you my rifle."

"Your choice. Thought I'd offer. My son has hard feelings. He'd rather take it off your body. Makes no difference to me."

Asa turned his head, just a little, as if he wanted to see if his friends had really deserted him, but thought better of it when Darnell lifted the barrel of his Spencer, a sparse but threatening move.

"I ain't takin' both of you on by myself." He eased down the hammer and allowed his rifle to slide to the ground.

"You're learning. Slow, but you're learning. Now unbuckle your belt and drop that short-gun."

As soon as the pistol hit the ground along with its holster and belt, Darnell said, "Now let's see your knife."

Asa pulled a skinning blade from his belt and dropped it. "Now we're quits." He lifted his reins.

"Not yet. Sail your hat over to my son."

"My hat?"

"Yeah, his got lost yesterday. I thought sure you'd bring it to him, but yours might do."

Asa jerked his hat off and threw it to the ground. Fane didn't move.

"You don't want that hat, son?"

"Seems he ought to hand it to me, Pa.

Wouldn't that be more polite?" Fane sounded mildly offended. Darnell figured his newly adopted son was beginning to enjoy himself.

"Get down and hand it to him, Asa. He thinks you ought to be more polite."

"I'll be damned if I will." Asa put both hands on the pommel of his saddle to hide the trembling.

"Being damned is a fearsome thing, Asa. It's a concern to us all from time to time, how we stand with the Man upstairs. You want to find out right now?" Darnell's rifle barrel drifted smoothly from the crook of his elbow to center on Asa's chest. "You want to find out now, or you want more time to do good deeds?"

"You wouldn't shoot a man after he downed his guns."

"You guess what I'll do while I decide."

Nolan shouted from where he'd stopped and turned his horse, "Mr. Baynes, we can't just ride off and let you shoot him down."

"Nolan, he's learning to be mannerly. If he learns, you have my word we won't shoot him."

Nolan's voice carried a clear edge of impatience. "For heaven's sake, Asa. Do what he wants, and let's get out of here. We got our horses back and a long way to go."

Asa slid from the saddle, and stood for a moment to steady himself. The man's knees wobbled under him. He jerked his hat off the ground, walked to Trampe, and offered it. Then he turned to Darnell and protested, "That's my new hat. His wasn't new."

Darnell ignored him. "Fit?"

Trampe answered without enthusiasm. "Fits all right, I guess. Cheap hat, Pa, but it's clean enough to wear."

"Cheap hat? That's a disappointment. How about that knife?"

Trampe walked over and picked up Asa's knife. "Nice blade." He sounded more pleased.

"Rifle?"

"It's as good as mine, Pa. Same kind. It'll do."

"Pistol?"

Trampe picked it up and examined it closely. "Piece of scrap. Rusted."

"Not a good trade, Asa. I know you want to be fair. What you got for boot?"

"What? Boot? You want boot? I guess you want the shirt off my back. You want that too?" Wild-eyed, Asa started unbuttoning his shirt.

When he stopped and looked at Darnell in disbelief, Darnell asked laconically, "You like that color, son?"

Trampe studied the garment. "Reminds me of dog shit, but I don't mind the color. Looks like it might fit. I could use it for a spare. Wouldn't want to wear it to town."

Asa turned to Darnell, his face tragic. He had stopped unbuttoning. "You going to take my shirt? I ain't even got another one with me."

Trampe corrected him. "We aren't taking anything from you, Asa. It's a trade. You're giving me the shirt in trade."

When Darnell's rifle muzzle bounced suggestively, the shirt came off. Asa handed it over.

Face flaming, Asa sprang into the saddle. "That's it. I ain't takin' no more from you. You can shoot me." He spurred toward his friends.

Darnell stood beside Trampe, neither speaking, until the horsemen vanished in the distance. Then Darnell turned to his "adopted son" and shook his head. "Sorry about that pistol. You carry my spare till we get to a town. I'll buy you a new one."

Trampe lifted both hands to his cheeks and bent over as if in pain, moving his feet in a clumsy dance. "I'm going to laugh if it tears my face off. You look at people and scare their drawers wet, just by looking at 'em and grinning. I got to watch how you do it. That was a marvel." He stopped his awkward victory dance and spoke apologetically. "Oh, about that pistol. Fine piece, Mr. Baynes. I was just rubbing his hair backwards. I'd never have figured him to be carrying a weapon fit for a real man."

After they mounted and headed south, Trampe spoke again. "You don't figure they'll try us again, do you? There were two more of them who didn't show."

"They left two behind to watch those stolen horses. No, they won't try us again. If they do, it'll be bad for them."

"Yes, sir. I think it will. I bet they know it too."

He handed Darnell's spare Navy back. "Obliged."

"Forget it."

Two hours later, when Darnell cast a curious glance at him, Trampe stopped his cheerful humming. He looked a bit sheepish, as if he'd been caught at something he wasn't aware of doing.

"You sound right cheerful, Fane. You getting over your aches and pains?"

"Yes, sir, feeling better. Doing some thinking, remembering back. Now I think I understand how your boys grew up so cocky."

"That so?"

"Yes, sir. I think I got it figured." He looked away and Darnell took that as a signal he wanted to say no more.

"Not to be a pest, Fane, but a man ought to test out new irons, get himself used to them."

"Yes, sir." He kicked his mount to a faster pace and pulled ahead. Without dismounting, he fired several shots from his new rifle and pistol. From the first, he showed easy proficiency with both weapons, the unmistakable confidence of those around guns from the cradle.

He reloaded and slowed to allow Darnell to overtake him. "Shooting a rifle sure don't help sore ribs."

They rode through the increasing heat of a clear day without further conversation. Nevada high desert has its own striking beauty, and it also has some of the most mind-deadening monotony on earth. From habit, Darnell spent his time looking for water, once in a while finding himself wearing a cynical smile. Man always looks for whatever is scarce. In the desert, he searches for water. In a swamp, he hunts for dry land. Settled, he yearns to wander. Roaming, he longs to settle.

After a while, Trampe started humming again.

Darnell rubbed his jaw while he pondered the sound. Maybe Trampe had found something scarce. He looked and sounded like a man pleased with his world. Maybe he'd found something he liked inside himself.

"Thought you might pop Asa one or two, just to return the favor."

"No pleasure in it, Mr. Baynes. Hitting a man under the gun is like hitting a man tied up."

"Yeah, about the same."

"Besides, hitting Asa would have messed up what you did."

"How's that?"

"You made him eat dirt in front of his friends. They'll carry that tale home with them."

"So?"

"If I'd have popped him one or two, it would've ruined the story. People would've felt sorry for him. Nobody laughs at somebody they feel sorry for. Asa will be hurt more by the snickers. Every time he sees his neighbors enjoy a joke, he'll think they're laughing at him."

"There's meanness in you, Fane."

"Sure is. Like you said, every man seeks his own kind of comfort."

"Did I say that?"

"Yes, sir."

EIGHT

Darnell watched Trampe unwind the rope from around his ribs. "Only been three days. You're a bit previous."

"I know I ain't healed yet, Mr. Baynes, but this rope itches me past bearing. I decided hurting is less of a grievance than wanting to scratch so bad it's making me crazy."

"You a drinking man like Micajah was? I carry a secret bottle for emergencies. Never thought to offer. I forget I have it."

"No thank you, sir. I find a little corn squeezing goes down nice now and again, but after Ma died, Pa got to where he liked his jug near to hand morning till night. It didn't help his thinking."

"I calculate we'll ride into Pioche today."

Trampe, still moving cautiously, shrugged back into his shirt. He took the rope he'd taken from around his body and worked it into a coil, hands quick and obviously accustomed to such tasks. "Maybe I can find work."

"You willing to work for me?"

"Yes, sir." The answer came quickly, as if he'd already given the idea thought and made the decision. Trampe dropped the coiled rope around the pommel of his grounded saddle and eased into a comfortable squat beside Darnell in the pale predawn light. He tapped the handle of the coffeepot to test its temperature before he lifted it to refill his cup. Darnell had already scattered the fire.

"You didn't ask what kind of work."

"No, sir. I didn't." When Darnell waited for him to say more, a brief silence fell. Finally, he added, "First time I been adopted. Seems like an orphan like me ought not to start out acting picky."

"I want you to take a job at the Raymond and Ely Mine. Act like a spy. See if you can find out if anything shady is going on."

Trampe remained motionless for several seconds except for one thumb idly rubbing his chin. "I ain't a miner. I hear working down in one of those holes pays good, but it's hell down in there. I thought you wanted me to work for you."

"You'll be spying for me. On second thought, maybe you wouldn't be a good miner. Can you drive a team? Could you handle an ore wagon?"

"Yes, sir. That's what I planned to do, as a matter of fact. I was heading this way when I took up with a horse thief without knowing it. Most any job sounds better than decorating a hay lift."

Again, conversation stopped while Darnell extended his cup and Trampe snagged the pot and filled it.

"Two questions come to mind, Mr. Baynes. Why do you want a spy in the Raymond and Ely Mine, and why do you care how much I drink?"

"I don't mind a drinking man, but I wouldn't like to hire one for dangerous work where one slip might be his last. There might be gunplay. One man has already died, shot in the back."

If young Trampe was going to take cards in the game, he deserved to know the risks. Fairness demanded telling him enough so he could protect himself. Darnell took a sip of coffee and started talking. Ten minutes later he asked, "You see what I'm up against?"

"No, sir. Sounds like you don't either. That's the main trouble, seems to me."

"I guess you're right."

Trampe lowered his cup to the ground and sat rubbing his hands together.

Darnell asked, "You got any ideas?"

Trampe took a deep breath and let it out slowly. "Some, maybe."

"Fire away."

"Mr. Baynes, I feel like a fool trying to give advice to you. You're the smart one sitting here right now. Went and got rich and all that. All my folks did was try to fight you and get ourselves killed."

"Man grows smart by listening. You through dodging yet? What's your thinking?"

Another deep breath, and Trampe spoke. "If I had sons like yours, they'd be with me right now. Nobody could shoot you in the back with them around. I been pondering on it. You scared hell out of those men who came after me, and I finally guessed why. You just didn't give a damn. Looked them in the eye and dared them to try something. Wasn't normal. They suspected right away you had somebody hid with a rifle aimed at them or something of that sort. That trick worked real good without you hardly trying. Otherwise, the way you were acting made no kind of sense. You got some reason to run at trouble rather than away from it?"

Darnell ignored the implication that his actions fell outside normal behavior. "My boys have families. They need to look after their own business."

Trampe lifted a hand sharply, like a man about to pound a table in frustration. The arm came back down slowly, and he started rubbing his hands together again. Darnell realized the hand rubbing signaled great tension in this young man. "Damn strange. Man can crook his finger and call an army to help him, but he won't. Those boys of yours could put the whole town of Pioche up a tree. All right. I guess you got your reasons, and they ain't really my business."

Darnell chuckled. "One day you'll have sons. You won't want to pester them with your problems."

Trampe didn't see the humor. "The hell I won't. When I have trouble I'll expect them to come a-running, belly to the sand."

"One day, maybe, we'll see. I'll remind you."

"Never mind that. Another thing, Mr. Baynes. You got an idea of snooping around and finding out what's going on without anybody knowing who you are? Well, that's just plain dumb. If I had any money, I'd bet it all you won't be in Pioche an hour without being picked out."

Darnell rose and went to his saddlebags. When he returned, he extended a fist, palm down. Trampe looked up, recognized the gesture, and stuck out a hand. The clink of gold coins sounded as loud as trace chains rattling in the cool desert stillness. "It's gun wages for dangerous work. One hundred dollars a month from me, and you keep whatever wages you earn when you get a job in town. That's your first month in advance."

"Too much money."

"You won't think so when you see how expensive everything is in a mining town."

"With this much money, I don't need to get a job. Best I hang around and watch your back."

"No, Fane, stay away from me unless you have something to tell me. Best we act like we don't know each other. Best we ride into town separately."

"Yeah, that's kind of familiar, I guess."

"What's familiar?"

"Sounds like all the stories about your family that float around in campfire gossip. Seems people only see one or two of you until trouble comes up. Then, all of a sudden, the river runs full of Bayneses, thick as a salmon run. I guess I'll have to learn how to watch out for you without people knowing what I'm up to."

"Oh, one other thing, Fane. Go to Perlman and Perlman freight office. Ask for Joshua Prime. Tell him I sent you. Tell him, if he can give you a job, I'll consider it a favor."

At Trampe's nod, Darnell came to his feet and lifted his saddle. "I'll go in first. Wait an hour or so before you come along."

Darnell's guess about the distance to Pioche missed the mark. He thought he might have to hurry to make it before nightfall, but the town came into sight a little before noon. He rode directly to a hotel, surprised to see such a grand structure in the slapdash double row of buildings. His surprise deepened when he stepped from the harsh light of the dusty street onto a clean carpet in the lobby. The hotel clerk's stiff expression eased into a smile when Darnell said, "Your best private room for a month."

A dubious inspection started at the floor with Darnell's battered boots and rose with insulting slowness to examine his grimy clothing, unshaven face, and sweat-stained hat. "Our rooms are five dollars a night, sir." The clerk made his statement sound the same as if he'd said "Go somewhere you can afford the rates, bum."

Darnell stacked eight double eagles on the counter and spun the register around. The clerk's hand lifted as if to snatch back the register, but he stopped instantly when he met

Darnell's eyes. Instead, he swept the gold coins into his hand and dropped them into a drawer.

When he offered a ten-dollar bill for change, Darnell said gently, "Don't offer me paper, man."

"It's perfectly good currency, sir."

Darnell figured his good nature had stood enough testing for one day. Having scrawled his name in illegible script on the register, he replaced the pen into the inkwell and placed both hands flat on the counter. He leaned forward and said, "I hate to repeat myself."

The clerk replaced the bill with a gold eagle and slid a key toward Darnell. He moved his hand quickly away from the key as if he'd die of cholera if Darnell touched him.

"Will you need a bellman to help you with your luggage, sir?"

The indirect inference that he had no luggage brought a grin to Darnell's face. He began to like this man. "I have trunks coming in to Wells Fargo, but I don't know if they've arrived yet. I'll tend to that myself."

Without waiting for a response, Darnell pocketed the key and turned away. At the hitching rail in front, he stripped off the saddle and pack from his horses. He stomped up the carpeted stairs, entered his room, and dropped his equipment to the floor. At the bed, he stripped back the covers and inspected for a full five minutes. If he found any sign of lice, he intended to dunk the hotel clerk in the nearest horse trough. All four bedposts rested in bowls of lamp oil, so somebody was trying to frustrate bedbugs. He found no traces and felt mildly disappointed. The clerk could have his next bath at his own convenience.

He led his horses down to the livery stable and ordered extra feed for them. Both animals showed too much rib. The graze along the route he had taken had varied from sparse to none, and the extra grain he'd brought on the pack horse hadn't fully made up for that.

He wandered back to the hotel porch and sat in the shade for a while, pleased to relax and watch the traffic. He wondered if motley mixtures of people existed in any other places like in a mining town. Blacks, Indians of unknown tribes in combinations of tribal and white man's garb, miners, saloon girls painted and dressed like tropical birds, wives in less vivid attire, gamblers in their uniforms of sober black, Chinese, prospectors, teamsters, con men, and speculators of every stripe drifted past. An occasional cowman rode by, never walking the sideboards, mounting to travel as far as the saloon next door. Dust blew and drifted, constantly working to blanket all colors but its own.

Darnell sat with his feet up on the hotel porch rail when a stage pulled up in front. His only response to the cloud of dust rolling over him was to lower his head to let his hat brim collect most of the grime. A fastidiously dressed man trotted across the street to open the stage door, and

Darnell found himself so dazzled he dropped his feet to the board floor and straightened in his chair to see better.

She eased down from the high stage step with the grace only possible with long, strong legs. Tall, probably only an inch or two less than six feet, she stood straight and proud, no slumping to try to look shorter. Hair pulled high under a wide-brimmed hat rimmed with cloth flowers in a rainbow of color only made her look taller. The bright colors emphasized her midnight black hair and eyes, in turn highlighted by an unblemished milk-white complexion. No farm girl this. She spread a parasol to block the sun the instant her feet touched the ground.

Chin high and shoulders back, she swung a cool gaze along the street with a single lofty, deliberate turn of her head. She looked for all the world as if she might consider buying this town if it measured up to her standards. Feeling the beginnings of a smile tug at his cracked lips, Darnell decided she only needed the right uniform to pose as a stretched big sister to Napoleon. He fumbled and searched for the right word and found it: statuesque. Amused with himself, he reflected that the word seemed appropriate so seldom a man shouldn't be surprised he had to fish for it when needed.

Darnell's amusement fed on itself when the short dandy greeted the grand Amazon. He probably stood about average height, but beside her, he seemed diminished. The little fellow at her elbow reminded Darnell of a circus boy trying to entice a lioness out of the arena and back into her cage. The poor fellow, bowing and mumbling his greetings, looked like he'd wet himself if she turned and snarled. At that moment, her drifting gaze met Darnell's over her companion's head, and she must have read his grin for what it was.

Eyes locked with his, she smiled, a companion's smile, born from the same unspoken private joke. Astonished, Darnell looked away quickly, feeling a hot rush to his face, not wanting to continue the contact for fear of staring like a rude schoolboy. Damned if she didn't look like she'd read his mind. Perfectly at ease a moment ago, he now felt a stab of self-consciousness.

His shirt was so rimed with salt and covered with grime and dust he'd forgotten the color. A hand drifted to his cracked lips and reminded him of several days' stubble. He saw himself in that awkward stage between clean-shaven and bearded, neither fish nor fowl, just unkempt. Thirty seconds ago it made no difference. Now he felt ashamed to be seen so scruffy.

"Here, you!"

At the commanding tone, Darnell looked up to find the dandy gesturing to him.

When he met Darnell's eyes, the dandy spoke in a more civil manner. "Help with this lady's luggage, will you? Be a good fellow. I'll pay you."

"Sure."

The stage driver stood on top of his rig, throwing aside tie-down ropes. When Darnell moved into the street beside the stage, the driver wrestled one end of a huge steamer trunk to the top of the guardrail and glanced down. "This trunk weighs half a ton, partner. It took four of us to get it up here."

"Ease it down."

He looked down at Darnell's heavy frame and shrugged. "Your funeral. I warned you. Catch it as soon as it starts tipping. I can't stop it once it starts to slide."

Darnell reached up, grabbed the wide leather handle on the end, and swung his shoulder under the huge trunk as it slid off the stage. Holding the forward edge tight against the back of his neck, he bent low under the leading end and flexed his knees, allowing the weight of the trunk to slide onto his back. The weight of the trailing end slid off the stage and down, bringing him almost upright. It balanced nicely, and he climbed the steps to the porch and into the hotel. The stage driver's shocked voice followed him inside. "Well, I'll be! Look at that."

He eased the trunk to the floor in front of the hotel desk and stood beside it. The Amazon came in with her escort trailing along. He said, "Thank you, that was well done, quite a feat of strength."

"You're welcome, glad to help." Darnell turned away, but her voice stopped him.

"Just a minute. Mr. Raymond offered to pay

you, I believe. It's my debt, not his." She extended a hand and Darnell, caught by surprise, did the same. She dropped a silver dollar into his palm.

"We need strong men around here. Are you, by chance, looking for work?" Raymond, when not standing too close to the Amazon, looked bigger.

"Just drifted in. Haven't decided yet."

"I'm the owner of the Raymond and Ely Mine. If you want a job, see one of my foremen. Tell them I sent you. I'll pass the word to expect you. By the way, I didn't catch your name."

Darnell hesitated briefly, then extended a hand. "I'm just called Nevada Darnell, Mr. Raymond."

Raymond nodded and looked at Darnell with sharpened interest. "Well, names aren't that important. Oh, I beg your pardon — Miss Fitzpatrick, may I introduce Mr. Darnell."

Darnell removed his shapeless hat and nodded, watching her gaze follow the dust that drifted toward the carpet from the brim of his Stetson. He caught a vagrant whiff of her perfume and shifted his feet to get a little more distance, thinking about his own fragrance, more than a week's collection of soured sweat, horse lather, gun oil, leather, dust, and tobacco. "Pleased to meet you folks. You must be eager to get to your room, ma'am, so I'll be moving along. Excuse me." Without waiting for a reply, he walked out the door.

He stopped immediately outside and leaned against the front wall. Their voices carried the short distance nicely.

The hotel clerk said, "A rather rough man, but he decided to stay here, even after he learned of our rates."

Raymond responded, a lilt of surprise in his voice. "He's a guest here?"

Miss Fitzpatrick laughed. "You sound astonished, Mr. Raymond. What's so surprising about that?"

"Nevada Darnell is not a name, Miss Fitzpatrick. It's an alias. He's obviously one of these Nevada toughs who hang around any place where money flows. Next week or next month, when the law comes too close, he'll be calling himself Texas Tom or Arizona Joe."

Darnell leaned against the wall, shamelessly eavesdropping and enjoying himself enormously.

The clerk's next comment came with a laugh. "We have all kinds of guests. No telling who some of the roughest-looking ones may turn out to be. Still, it'll be interesting to see if he shows up in the dining room tonight, looking like he just finished mucking out a stable."

Darnell eased off the side of the hotel porch and drifted down the street, chuckling to himself. He wished he could be a fly on the wall and watch that desk clerk figure a way to get that monster of a trunk upstairs. It had taken every ounce of strength he'd had to avoid buckling under the weight of the damn thing. Had he not learned how to balance such weights from friendly Negro stevedores in New Orleans as a boy, he'd probably be prostrate in the dust right now with men trying to get him out from under it. That trunk probably weighed as much as a small piano.

He had two notions of what he'd like to do. One, go roll in the muck pile behind the nearest stable and appear in full fragrance for dinner at their snooty hotel dining room. Two, go to the barber shop and get himself cleaned, polished, and a light coat of oil applied.

He pulled out the silver dollar Miss Fitzpatrick had given him. It arced high in the air and fell into his ready palm. He slapped the coin down on the opposite wrist and set the rules. Heads, to the muck pile. Tails, to the barber shop.

The flicker of a coin in the air attracted attention. A couple of black-garbed gamblers stopped and grinned at him, instant brothers in the world of chance. He stood for a few more seconds, coin trapped between right hand and left wrist. They waited. He took a peek. Tails. The barber shop won.

One of the gamblers asked, "Come out good?"

Darnell returned the smiles from the two curious men and responded, "I don't know. I'm kinda disappointed. I wanted to do something real silly, but the grown-up choice won."

One gambler snapped his fingers in sympathy.

His companion said, "There's always another day. The best of us can have a bad run." They walked away with a laugh and a friendly wave.

Darnell pondered a moment. Now he'd have to pick up his two trunks of clothes at Wells Fargo and lay out some of his formal attire. Even if he had trapped himself into following a sensible course, the temptation to kick up his heels persisted. The only thing he could do now, since his new coin trapped him into acting like a mature person, was to go the opposite direction. He'd overdress. Yeah. By golly, he'd go dressed up like Little Lord Fauntleroy. He'd swagger around and try to act cordial to the lower class of people who had sense enough to come eat their evening meal wearing comfortable clothes.

He'd spotted the Wells Fargo office when a new thought came to him. The heaviness of his step had dropped away. Life has its wonders. One beautiful woman smiles at him on the street and Darnell Baynes runs to climb into his best clothing. She qualified as the prettiest creature he'd seen in years. Tonight would be fun. She probably wouldn't remember him, wouldn't even look in his direction. Didn't matter. He'd find a way to catch her attention if he had to spit in the punch bowl to do it.

An hour and a half later, he sat in a tub of hot water, feeling comfortable and drowsy, when yet another thought struck him. Raymond introduced her as Miss Fitzpatrick. He'd been so inattentive he hadn't put it together. The stockholder who got shot in the back had been a Fitzpatrick.

Tall woman, fine figure, walked with a nice athletic grace, lively, alert, an interesting Amazon. Walked and dressed like royalty. And she was named Fitzpatrick. It could be coincidence, but Darnell didn't believe that for a second.

He remembered one sparkling spring day, seemed like it was Easter. The Baynes clan rode through a little town in Nebraska just as church let out. They reined their horses to a halt to allow three young women, generously endowed and dressed in their bright new gowns, to cross the street in front of them. His sons devoted rapt attention to the crossing girls, who in turn giggled and shot sideways glances at the entranced horsemen. After their horses had moved down the street a hundred feet or so, none of the boys daring to look back for fear of rough teasing from the others, Luke, the man of fewest words, said in his matter-of-fact way, "Sure is a pleasure to see girls grow up so healthy."

Darnell laughed, causing the bath water to surge around the tub. Luke would certainly agree. Miss Fitzpatrick had grown up looking mighty healthy indeed.

NINE

Darnell walked to the head of the carpeted stairway with smug self-confidence. He paused there a moment, musing.

Years had flown by, but he'd forgotten nothing. The aristocratic and socially prominent Silvana family of New Orleans, forced to tolerate him, wanted to avoid as much embarrassment as possible. The rough young man who had eloped with one of their daughters had been tutored. Their hirelings coached him until his manners had been judged to he flawless. Not merely acceptable — flawless.

His response had awed the arrogant Rodrigo Silvana, the reluctant brother-in-law, into first respect, then admiration, and finally a deep and abiding friendship. Darnell still marveled at the change.

This same man had strapped on a pistol, determined to kill Darnell Baynes for eloping with his sister. But he had been traveling abroad when the unacceptable marriage took place. By the time he returned, his beloved but misguided and headstrong sister had already conceived, and he had reluctantly stayed his hand. Rodrigo, fiery-tempered but of enormous intellectual capacity himself, had become fascinated with the fact that Darnell Baynes never needed to be told anything twice.

Violating his usual coldly condescending manner, he had commented one day, "Mr. Baynes, you have a masterful memory, simply extraordinary. I've never seen such concentration. You act like your life depends on learning all these little niceties."

"It does."

"Whatever does that mean?"

"Your sister wants me to learn."

"Well, yes, I understand she does, but that doesn't explain this kind of grim determination."

"She gave up a lot to marry me, Mr. Silvana. It's the only thing she asked of me. I promised. Now I've got to do it, sir. Nobody who breaks faith in his own home can have a good life."

Rodrigo Silvana, erect, haughty, ever conscious of his aristocratic forebears and wealth, stood motionless for a long time, so long his cigar burned dangerously close to his fingers. Then, as if awakening, he abruptly said, "Please call me Rod," and excused himself.

That night, Maria told Darnell with wonder in her voice, "Rodrigo came to me today. My arrogant big brother approached me as if I were an avenging angel. I've never seen him act humbled before, never in my life. He said he would be forever in my debt if I would forgive him for the many unkind and insulting things he said about you in the past. I was stunned. The only thing I could think of to say was 'Forgiveness is never free. It must be earned.' You know how formally he always talks. He said that was imminently fair, and he proposed to begin without delay. Darnell, what on earth could have changed him so?"

Darnell, half asleep, said comfortably, "All Spaniards are insane," and got a Spanish woman's fist to the ribs.

"Excuse me."

Darnell snapped out of his reverie and stepped aside. "I beg your pardon, ma'am. I didn't intend to block the stairs."

She swept past but paused after descending three or four steps and turned back. "I beg your pardon. I didn't recognize you, but I think I remember your voice. Didn't we meet this afternoon?"

"Yes, Miss Fitzgerald." A minor little jab. He didn't want her to think he took particular notice.

"It's Fitzpatrick." Her cool response showed no spark. The jab missed.

"Of course. I beg your pardon. May I ask your given name, ma'am. It might help me to remember."

"I am Rosalinda Ozuna Fitzpatrick."

"A pleasure, ma'am. Your name has a certain musical ring to it."

"And you make up a new name wherever you go, don't you? I'm told that's the custom among many Nevada toughs. What shall I call you this evening?"

"I was a Nevada tough this afternoon, but I've had a bath. Did wonders for me. Since I washed most of Nevada off, I'd suggest you forget that part and just call me Tough. Of course, you could call me dear, or sweetheart, or some affectionate name like that. It sounds friendly."

A smile flashed and vanished, a brief assent to his attempt at wit. "I do believe you're teasing me. Why should I bother to sound friendly to a man I hardly know, Mr. Tough Darnell?"

He came down the steps to stand beside her and offered his arm. "Nevada Darnell is just the traveling name I use. May I escort you to dinner, Miss Fitzpatrick?"

Her eyes flickered and she hesitated. "That's a flattering invitation, sir, but I'm to join several gentlemen this evening. A dinner has been arranged to introduce me to several business associates."

"I understand. I shall be honored to escort you to their table and withdraw."

She took his arm, and they descended the stairs slowly. She looked up at him with a smile. "You use a traveling name? Whatever for?"

"Convenience. My real name disturbs some people." His plan wasn't working. He'd been repeatedly advised it wouldn't, and he shouldn't have stubbornly persisted. Besides, his selection of a false name was poorly thought out. It would be accepted without question at a cow camp or a mine hiring line, but it was too obviously a dodge among moneyed people. It only aroused curiosity. Time to drop the whole charade. "I'm Darnell Baynes."

She came to a stop several steps short of the hotel lobby and turned wide black eyes on him, direct as the beam of a bull's-eye lantern. "Are you the infamous Darnell Baynes, the outlaw from Louisiana?"

By heaven, she knew how to test a man's temper, calling him infamous to his face. "Partly right, Miss Fitzpatrick. I'm from Louisiana, but I'm not an outlaw. I'm a businessman. Few things have come to me in my life that I didn't work for, but infamy came without my earning it."

"Reputations, both men's and women's, can be damaged easily." Her gaze dropped to his hand, exposed when he proffered an arm on which she rested a light hand. He followed the glance and saw the flaw through her eyes. Two hours of barbering, shaving, and bathing, the expensively tailored clothes, the diamond stickpin, the oval gold cufflinks with half-carat diamonds sparkling in their centers — all were rendered ineffective by one cool glance from this woman. None of these frills hid the heavily callused, sun-darkened hand with its scarred knuckles and thick fingers. He felt like a man whose hairpiece had slipped. The pretense became ludicrous.

He wore no rings, trying to avoid drawing attention to his hands, which usually succeeded.

His hands came nowhere close to the tapered grace typical of the wealthy or aristocratic. No elegant disguise could survive such a glaring defect. He had to resist an absurd impulse to cover his hand with the other. Her kind of people simply didn't accept that a gentleman worked with his hands. It was unthinkable.

Darnell almost flinched with shock when she covered the weather-beaten hand with her own, as if she'd heard his thought spoken aloud. She chuckled, a soft and intimate sound, and said in a low voice, almost a whisper, "I can almost hear your mind turning, Mr. Baynes. I suspect you are giving me too much credit for a simple observation. No man could display such strength as you did this afternoon without working hard for it."

"I hope I'm not interrupting." Raymond, standing at the foot of the stairs, looked up and smiled.

Darnell took the last stairs to the lobby and dropped his arm, the universal signal of the end of his escort formality. He bowed in greeting and smiled, an effort to disguise a sting of irritation. He couldn't decide whether it sprang from the interruption or from having allowed himself to become so engrossed with the woman that someone could approach unnoticed.

"Good evening, Mr. Raymond. Mr. Baynes and I met by chance in the hall. He was kind enough to escort me down the stairs."

Raymond offered his arm and she took it. "Baynes? Did you say Baynes?"

"Yes, I'm Darnell Baynes. I often use a traveling name." Darnell smiled as if caught in a mild peculiarity.

Raymond's eyes narrowed briefly. "A coincidence, perhaps. A rather large stockholder in my mine has the same last name. A partnership, if I remember correctly, with TBI on the letterhead."

"Thackery and Baynes Investments, Mr. Raymond. I'm the Baynes part of that."

Raymond threw up his hands. The surprised gesture freed his arm from Miss Fitzpatrick's hand. "I didn't know you were coming, sir. Had I known, I would have properly greeted you. Please join us for supper. I've asked some of our supervisory staff to meet Miss Fitzpatrick this evening."

"Oh? The lady wants to meet mining men?"

"Yes. Miss Fitzpatrick has become a stockholder. She suffered a tragic loss recently and inherited valuable property."

Darnell turned to her. "I heard a man named Fitzpatrick was killed here recently. Was he a relative of yours, Miss Fitzpatrick?"

"My stepbrother."

"My condolences. I'm deeply sorry."

"Thank you, Mr. Baynes. He was much older than me, and I'm afraid he never approved of his father's marriage to my mother. Frankly, I was shocked to learn he left his property to me, but he had no other family."

Darnell tucked away the question about ownership of Fitzpatrick's stock. He'd solved that mystery simply by engaging in small talk in a hotel lobby.

"Please." Raymond gestured toward the dining room. "Come join us, Mr. Baynes. We'll set another place with no trouble at all."

"I wouldn't think of intruding, but thank you."

"Nonsense. Come along. I think dinner is about to be served. We'll just have time for introductions."

Darnell followed them into the dining room. When they approached a large table, three men rose to greet them. Raymond conducted the introductions, and Darnell used his old power of concentration to commit the names and faces to memory. John Ely particularly interested him. A big man, standing about six feet, almost as tall as Darnell, he carried extra flesh well in spite of an overly sanguine coloring. Bluff and hearty, he quickly showed why he had the reputation as the spokesman for the Raymond and Ely partnership. Few men could monopolize conversation as smoothly as Ely. The smaller and less flashily dressed William H. Raymond was regarded as the clever dealer and sharp miner.

The other two men seemed ill at ease. Both were dressed in less expensive, untailored business suits. Darnell noted their accents and judged them to be Welshmen. If so, they belonged to a group reputed to be the best hard rock miners in the world. Small and wiry, they were introduced as the supervisors of the day and night shifts.

The evening passed uneventfully, a relaxed and enjoyable social occasion, with all the men paying close attention to the only lady present. Darnell detected no signal that Raymond and Ely recognized that he and this striking woman owned enough shares to take control of the mine. If that fact bothered them, both concealed their concern effectively.

Miss Fitzpatrick seemed perfectly at ease without the presence of other ladies. Darnell figured she would attract the attentions of men even if the room had been crowded with other females. Fully mature, she must be thirty or so. He found it odd that a woman of her beauty and social grace would remain a spinster. She must suffer from a serious imperfection not yet revealed.

He stayed alert all evening, but the conversation dwelt on trivial matters of no interest to him. He excused himself as early as possible and retired to his room. Once there, he shucked his grand garments, snuffed the lamp, and sat at a small writing table to smoke a cigar.

He'd seen no sign of Trampe. Nothing hindered him from using Darnell's hundred dollars for traveling money to leave the country if he chose, but Darnell didn't credit that possibility. Trampe could be found somewhere in Pioche at this very moment. Darnell would bet money on it. He chuckled at the thought. He had already bet a hundred dollars.

Pure chance had provided him two potentially useful allies, Trampe and Prime.

Darnell, sitting in a dark room at a careful distance from the open window, smiled at himself. He had no real reason to worry about someone trying a shot at him through that window, yet ingrained caution ruled. Fitzpatrick probably hadn't had a reason to expect a bullet in the back either.

Here he sat, without anything resembling a real plan to detect thieving if it occurred, and his mind kept circling back to the woman.

A man who couldn't face himself honestly lived with an irreparable handicap. No sense ducking the truth. That was one fascinating woman. She aroused a kind of response in him he'd thought had died with Maria. How long ago? Eight years? Nine? Whatever, it was a long time for part of a man to lie dormant and still assert itself again so suddenly with all its power.

He didn't need this foolishness. He could make a buffoon of himself easily enough without suffering through a recurrence of juvenile passion. All he had to do was show a little strength of character. He'd ignore the damn woman and go about his business.

That settled, he went to the window and stood beside it for a moment to ensure the street outside was empty. He pitched out the still-smoking cigar. He'd enjoyed it, but he didn't want to wake up with it in the room in the morning. Dead cigars gave out an evil odor powerful enough to turn a man green in the morning. He eased himself into bed and lay staring at the ceiling.

Damned if he'd ignore her. If she took an interest in handsome, urbane Darnell Baynes, it would be unkind to ignore her. She was probably lying awake right now scheming up ways to get his attention. He'd better be prepared to help her divert her unseemly and unladylike passion into more acceptable pursuits.

An explosive guffaw burst from him before he could strangle it, and he lay giggling and snorting like a perfect idiot for several seconds. Finally under control again, he lay in his bed smirking. He thought he might be a bit young for it, but a man endured his second childhood when it chose to afflict him, not at a time he picked. He didn't feel old, but he must be growing silly. If so, he might as well enjoy it as much as any other part of his life. Smiling, he turned on his side and went to sleep.

A single light tap on the door brought him to instant alertness. He rolled from the bed, lifting his Navy from the holster and belt draped across the nearby chair. He approached the door on silent bare feet and stood aside from it before answering in a low tone. "Yes?"

No answer. He waited several seconds, shifted to the other side of the door, and answered again. "Yes?"

Muffled noise from the street filtered into the silence of the hotel. Pioche never really slept. Like the shore of the Pacific, the sound of movement in boisterous mining towns rose and fell but never quieted completely.

He stood listening with all his might, but whoever tapped on his door either slipped away light-footed or still stood perfectly motionless in the hall. The errant thought that he'd imagined the sound crept around the edge of his mind, and he roughly dismissed it. He trusted his own senses above all else. Of all the damn fool questions he'd ever heard in his life. "Did you hear something too?" qualified as the stupidest. A man either heard something or he didn't. It made no difference whether someone else heard it.

A city man might open that door and look around. A city man might get himself shot for careless curiosity. Darnell's kind of man would wait. If someone wanted him, it was up to them. They could tap again or go away. Their choice.

Then he saw something on the floor. Oblong, with squared corners, almost the same shade as the floor in the heavy shadows. Someone had slipped a dark envelope under his door. The tap Darnell had heard must have been the slightest touch of the visitor's fingers when pushing the envelope all the way under. Whoever slipped him a message didn't want even a corner of the envelope to be visible from the hall.

He squatted beside the door and drew the envelope slowly to him with the barrel of the Navy. He drew in a cautious deep breath and caught a faint aroma. Perfume? Scented paper, by heaven, and he recognized the fragrance.

He retreated slowly to the dresser and fumbled a match from his pants pocket. The flap of the envelope wasn't sealed. He opened it without sound, unfolded the letter inside, and struck the match. He read the message with a quick glance and blew out the match. He remained in the corner until his eyes recovered from the brief burst of light.

Tough,
Meet me for breakfast. Seven-thirty.
Linda

Fancy handwriting but easy to read. All kinds of pretty swirls and loops. What did they call it? Calligraphy.

His Navy replaced in its holster and himself back in bed, he stared at the ceiling wide awake again. The letter under his nose, he explored it. Not perfumed stationery. The fragrance came from one isolated spot. She'd touched a finger, dipped in her perfume, to the paper in one spot directly under the signature. Could that sharp-eyed woman know she dealt with a backwoods man with keenly honed senses? If so, she'd devised an unusual way to authenticate her signature.

Just Linda. Not Rosalinda. Not Miss Fitzpatrick. Another clue. After their verbal fencing around with his name, she'd picked a way to alert him to the name she preferred, and it was her first name. No, even better, it was a diminutive, an informal shortening of her first name. Did this carry an implied invitation to use it, a bold gesture indeed on such short acquaintance? Seemed mighty likely. He'd test it, if they managed to breakfast alone.

TEN

Heavy drapes, closed in the evenings, had been drawn back to invite the morning light. Darnell walked to where the Amazon sat at a table alone, erect, a touch of haughtiness in her bearing that invited no company in a room almost full.

"Good morning."

She nodded without answering, a hint of a smile her only sign of recognition, a courteous expression, as if in polite enquiry to a stranger as to what he might want.

He hesitated, struck by a last-minute suspicion that she might have delivered the note on impulse last night and changed her mind later. "I believe I was invited to join you."

"You were." She used a flat tone, more like she was verifying he'd obeyed instructions correctly than acknowledging he'd responded to an invitation.

He took a seat beside her and leaned in her direction, careful to get close enough to speak in a low tone but not so near as to appear familiar. "Linda suits you. Lovely name for a lovely woman."

"I prefer Miss Fitzpatrick when we can be overheard."

"That's fine. Some things are best not shared."

"Don't get the wrong idea. I think it would profit us to appear to be friends. Nothing more." Her cool, dismissive manner lacked even routine social warmth. An invitation to "appear" to be friends, issued in her tone of voice, implied that real friendship fell beneath her icy dignity.

He decided to test the ice. "I've been riddled with wrong ideas since the moment I saw you, Amazon. Your note set me to dreaming all night. Now you crush my fantasy with one brutal comment. See me shrinking? Never has a man been deflated so quickly."

"Amazon?" She lifted a brow, no trace of amusement in her direct gaze.

"Yes, ma'am, warrior women so beautiful their enemies forgot to fight and died happy. That's the first word that popped into my mind when you stepped off that stage. The second was statuesque."

"I invited you here to talk business. If you have idle flirtation in mind, you are wasting my time."

"Talk business after we eat." He unfolded his napkin and draped it across his lap when he saw the waiter approaching. Early in his training he'd been told that waiters would sometimes grandly place a napkin in a customer's lap as a way to pretend to serve but actually to deliver insult.

They ordered, and the waiter departed. Darnell said, "We need not ruin a good meal with business. You wanted us to be seen together. Let's be sure to tarry so nobody misses the show. Those you want to see us may not be early risers."

She met his gaze without the least waver. "I knew you'd see that right away, so you needn't be self-righteous. I didn't underestimate you."

"I'm not self-righteous. I'm too busy picking up the pieces of my shattered fantasies to be righteous about anything."

"I thought it might provide advantage for us to be seen together, to appear to be allies. Between us, we own enough shares to exercise control of the mine. I assume you're aware of that."

"A good subject to discuss after breakfast."

"Mr. Baynes, you have a playful manner this morning I find unnerving. I shouldn't have written that note. You presume too much."

"All the way back to Mr. Baynes, is it? Why don't you just call me Tough. All us toughs are playful." The woman seemed determined to treat him like a subordinate, and an acid feeling of hostility began to eat at him.

The waiter arrived with their breakfast, and conversation stopped until he walked away.

She spoke firmly but without heat, a schoolmistress instructing a misbehaving student. "Mr. Baynes, I warn you, I have been treated in a cavalier fashion by many men. Most have regretted that later. If you intend to treat me like an empty-headed woman, we have no need to talk further."

"I'm treating you like a beautiful woman. You may forget the condition nature forced on you, but that kind of forgetfulness is against my character. That's the way it's going to be unless you prove to be as sour and stern as that last remark sounded. The emptiness of your head remains to be discovered. Your lack of a sense of humor saddens me."

She placed her fork carefully on her plate and turned to face him. It looked like the breakfast talk had about reached its end. Darnell inwardly shook his head. Too bad. Some people aren't meant to get along with each other. A sudden sense of disappointment blew through him like a gloomy wind.

"I don't like being lectured to."

He shrugged. "No charge."

She hesitated, fingers of both hands on the edge of the table as if prepared to rise.

Darnell looked her in the eye. "Go ahead. Prove you're a flighty, empty-headed spinster. Run away."

Her fingers lost some of their tension, and she relaxed in her seat, both movements so carefully controlled they probably weren't visible from the next table. Darnell figured she had reached the point where she'd sit there till she died rather than give him cause to think he'd made her run.

Darnell kept his voice low and flat. "You'll never grow big and strong unless you finish your meals. Amazons have to eat hearty."

"This rough teasing is out of place. You're acting like a damn fool." The Amazon's voice remained low and perfectly cool, but he felt a flame of rage behind her iron control. Darnell knew his own expression didn't vary, but he felt a sense of wonder. The woman was furious. What could have set her afire? Her eyes were hard and black as onyx, but her face displayed no tension. She wore a socially correct blank face like a mask, even showing a slight smile.

"I love the way you curse. Some ladies never get the hang of it."

"You son of a . . ."

"Why did you stop? Want me to guess the last word? Give me a hint. Does it start with a *b* as in baby?"

"You came down here just to bait me, didn't you?"

"No. Truth is, I came down here to find out if you had a brain. If you proved out to be clever enough, I planned to ask you to be my partner. I think we're both getting cheated." He tabled his fork and took a sip of coffee. "I'm finished eating and ready to talk business. I'll wait for you to clean your plate."

"I'll not sit here and be ordered to clean my plate. I'm not a child."

A petty, spiteful remark. Looking for insult behind every idle conversational gambit signaled an unstable, defensive attitude. "If you can't tell the difference between a pleasant invitation and an order . . ." He left the comment unfinished, shrugged, and looked away with a show of real indifference. He had just about lost hope for anything useful to come from this meeting.

She picked up her fork. "I did underestimate you. I thought you might be — I didn't expect you to be so offhand and carefree about serious questions involving huge amounts of money. In fact, I thought you might be a little slow and awkward. You were almost mute at dinner last night. Do most outlaws have such a love for nonsense?"

"I'm unique. I'm not even an outlaw."

"What makes you think we're being cheated?"

"The same thing that makes you think so."

"Falling profits? My stepbrother's murder?"

"We think alike. Again, my sincere sympathies about your brother."

"I expected another of your clever remarks, but that sounded sincere. Have you finally decided to talk seriously?"

"I'm feeling better about us. Our first lovers' quarrel ended by the time we finished our breakfast. Good. It's best to argue at breakfast. Gives us all day to get over it." Her insistence on acting insulted at every implication they could be friends gave him a perverse delight in teasing her. "The first order of business will be the requirement to keep you alive."

"You think I'm in danger?"

"Yes. I think we should conduct our investigation together. I have no friends or employees here, so I can only offer you my personal protection. I do suggest, though, that we visit the marshal. He might send a deputy to look after you, pretty as you are."

She threw up her hands, only a twitch of movement, a sparse signal. It probably equaled a less controlled woman throwing her plate on the floor. "You cannot stop. You simply will not stop. You have to stick a joke into everything that comes out of your mouth."

"Joke?"

"That 'pretty as you are' remark. The tasteless remark before that about our first lovers' quarrel."

Darnell leaned forward and tapped the table for emphasis. "Pretty for a woman is as good as a rifle for a man. It's a weapon that should always be treated like it's loaded. By the way, can you shoot too?"

She thought for a second before she shook her head. That little pause said she lied. She almost surely had a weapon somewhere, probably in her handbag, and he'd bet a week's work she knew how to use it.

"Then let's play the helpless pretty woman card and see if we can shuffle help out of the law."

"You do know how to turn a clever phrase, Darnell."

"You must remember not to call me that in front of other women. Jealousy springs up everywhere I go."

"Some things are best not shared."

He paused at her comment, realized it sounded familiar, and gave her a look. She met his gaze with false innocence. Damned if she hadn't thrown his own words back at him. Maybe she had a trace of humor hidden away somewhere after all.

"I don't really have a plan. All I've got in mind is to snoop around and try to find out if something is really wrong and then figure out what to do about it. What's your plan?"

She eyed him openly, her gaze hard and searching. "I'm not sure I trust you enough to tell you. I have no experience with outlaws. You needn't hide your hands. I've already seen them."

Her change of subject, almost in mid-sentence, threw him for a moment. He didn't move his hands, resting on his knees, concealed under the table. That remark had only one purpose, to put him in his place, to put him on the defensive.

"Just a habit."

He took his time considering his next remarks, letting the silence between them build into a tense breach in the conversation. He decided to end this discussion, and he wanted to do it with a lasting closure, a clean break that prevented another like it.

The word of a Baynes was known to be good as gold, outlaw myth or not. To be told to his face he was not trusted struck deep. Her remark equaled a slap in the face. If she had been a man, he would probably have struck her. The only decent thing about the insult was its privacy. Thank heaven she hadn't thrown that remark at him in front of anyone else. Throughout their conversation he had been leaning slightly toward her so they could talk in low tones. Now he relaxed and sat back in his chair.

"You've been honest about not trusting me. Trust must be earned, and I've had no chance to do that. I'll not deny being an outlaw in your presence again. You've made it plain you don't believe me, so it's wasted breath. You have a plan, I guess, that has to be kept secret to work. Keep your secrets. I'll keep my protection. I didn't welcome the burden of looking after you anyway, and I shouldn't have offered. Having a man you don't trust hanging around would test the patience of a saint. There's no need for us to work together. Both of us got along fine without the other up to now. No need to change."

Her lip curled, a careful, controlled expression. "Now you expect me to apologize and beg for your help."

"Without trust, we can't work together. I expect nothing from you, nothing at all."

"What you're really saying is that I can expect nothing from you. Isn't that right, Mr. Baynes?"

"Exactly." He dropped his napkin on his plate and signaled the waiter. Perfect. He'd been a little windy, but he'd burned the bridges down to the water level.

"You were my guest, Mr. Baynes. I invited you. I shall pay."

"As you wish. Thank you. Excuse me." No call to quibble over nickels and dimes. He rose, bowed formally, and walked back up to his room for his hat. When he passed through the foyer again, he glanced into the dining room. She still sat at the breakfast table, staring out the window. Her straight posture and squared shoulders were haughty and unbending as ever, but something about her stillness struck him as painfully lonely.

Darnell paused before stepping through the front door and smoothed his newly brushed hat. It didn't look too bad now that a quarter inch of dust had been knocked off. The Amazon reacted with rage at the simple little teasing remarks common between men and women everywhere. Men were expected to act and talk as if every woman they met inspired dreams and worshipful admiration, wore the most beautiful gown in town, danced better than any princess from Paris. Her apparent resentment of a harmless social convention seemed odd and mean-spirited.

He searched his mind for similar harsh responses from women. He remembered none, but he'd had no business dealings with them. In fact, now that he pondered on it, he usually hit it off fine with women. Yet, everything he said stirred a swarm of furies behind Miss Fitzpatrick's eyes.

He chuckled to himself. He didn't even presume to call her Linda in his thoughts. No wonder she had grown into a spinster. Vinegar attracts no flies, and a sour apple is unwelcome in any barrel. Still, by some trick of nature, she was a pretty thing, a stunner by his lights. He slapped on his hat and walked out into the street.

Rosalinda Ozuna Fitzpatrick sat staring through the dining room window with sightless eyes, burning with fury.

She breathed deeply and regularly, making herself calm down. She hadn't committed an error this profoundly awkward in years. Darnell Baynes, a common outlaw with a blacksmith's hands and the strength of a goliath, had fooled her. Her estimate of the man had been dead wrong.

The gentleness in his eyes when she'd touched his hand last night misled her. His quiet demeanor at dinner reinforced the error. Big men frequently had a soft center, a timidity around women, that she'd used to advantage more times than she could count. She'd seen the spark of interest in him, and she'd calculated him to be vulnerable, easy to command, eager to please.

Darnell Baynes didn't seem to care if the mine played out tomorrow. He certainly didn't care if Linda Fitzpatrick fell down a well. Behind his studied bluff and jovial teasing manner, she'd seen, too late, a coldly calculating mind at work.

When she'd planned to draw him out by implying she didn't trust him, she thought he'd try to justify himself, and that would put her in the position of leadership, the one to be satisfied, the one in control. Instead, he dismissed her like an apprentice maid. He'd looked straight into her eyes with imperious indifference. Aside from trivial departing comments, the interview suffered an abrupt termination worthy of aloof royalty. She had disqualified herself from further consideration.

As a last ploy, her offer to pay for breakfast should have made him pause, touched his pride, given her a moment to recover and to smooth the situation. He didn't care who paid. A lesser man would have pulled money and dropped it on the table or some other grand gesture. Only now, sitting in a suffocating cloud of frustration, did she understand the depth of his indifference. He forgot her before he reached the door.

After seething through an uncomfortable and tiring trip to get here, mind focused on vengeance, a plan had exploded into her mind last night. Fitz said in his last letter that an alliance with the California firm, TBI, might be the answer. Fitz believed Raymond and Ely were honest, as honest as mine owners can be in a cutthroat world, but incompetent in the small but critical details of good management. Fitz thought their hired managers had devised a way to siphon off profits.

Poor Fitz. Her eyes stung for a moment, but she forced them to stay dry with sheer force of will. Her gentle stepbrother had been clever but no fighting man. Why did a murderer bother to shoot him from behind when Fitz never even went armed?

She forced herself to think about her failed plan. It had seemed perfect. The fortuitous appearance of rough-hewn Darnell Baynes seemed a gift from the gods of chance, a big, strong, slow man she could wrap around her finger. Control of the mine seemed a foregone conclusion with Baynes eager to do her bidding. More importantly, he might be the perfect tool to avenge Fitz. The law regarded his death as just another back-alley murder, and that seemed routine here.

Worst of all, she'd found herself interested, and that made her angry with herself, and that clouded her thinking. His blunt fingers handled cutlery with the delicacy and mastery of long acquaintance. Every move last night and this morning displayed unthinking, habitual grace of movement and conduct. The other men at the dining table last night had not been clumsy or unrefined, but Baynes made them appear unpolished. This impression, coming from a man who handled a two-hundred-fifty-pound trunk without assistance, formed a seeming paradox interesting to anyone.

She couldn't — wouldn't — allow herself to take interest in another man. Never again. Sooner or later, the rancid old rumor would reach his ears. Then the doubt would come into his eyes, and she would dismiss him, her pride wounded again.

Like a blow from behind, Darnell's comment came back to her. "Without trust, we can't work together." Exactly why she had dismissed one suitor after another. Her pride couldn't tolerate their doubts in the face of an ugly rumor. Now, she had been dismissed for the same reason, her own lack of trust, revealed out of her own mouth. She'd stupidly caused her own downfall.

Perhaps she might arrange another chance with this man. Next time, she would make it clear that he was to be the leader. She would guide his thinking, of course. She had no other contacts with the kind of men she could use to avenge Fitz.

Linda Fitzpatrick rubbed the side of her cheek and tried to conjure up an approach. After this morning, she'd have to be clever indeed. Great damage had been done. She caught herself frowning and forced a slight smile. Frown lines destroyed a woman's face.

Darnell could be compared to a wild bear. Success in controlling him would always be doubtful. He would forever be dangerous and unpredictable. But he would know outlaws; he might know at this very moment who killed Fitz. Thinking about Darnell Baynes tightened something inside her, so she resumed her deep, measured breathing. She realized her smile had become real.

Perhaps, if nothing else, the Amazon and the Tough might entertain each other for a while in this gritty little town. He had a rather droll sense of humor she'd been too intense to appreciate. Another mistake. She must make herself relax, control that driving energy that repelled men.

Amazon indeed. That remark shook her badly for a moment. Was her grim determination to find and punish whoever killed Fitz obvious to him? No, he'd been simply referring to her size. Somehow, probably just by chance, the man had touched on one subject after another in such a manner as to keep her off balance.

Her height alienated many men, but he made it sound like her best feature. Darnell towered over her and, oddly, she found that comfortable for a change. She seldom met men taller than she was, and it usually irritated her to look up at them.

Darnell Baynes, according to rumor a man widely traveled, a widower with sons grown into alert and quick-tempered men, a leader of an outlaw clan the law never touched, a man of wealth, a partner in an investment company with diverse holdings, didn't sound like the perfect person to be duped like a simple rube. After he left the table last night, the men gossiped about him worse than a ladies' sewing circle.

They tried to top each other with stories about the legendary Baynes clan.

Linda's bitterness became such a physical reality her mouth turned sour. She took a sip of cold coffee. The more she considered what she'd been told about Darnell Baynes, the more her mistake this morning seemed unthinkable. She wondered if all she heard could be true about one man. A tantalizing sense of latent energy around him caused her to suspect the rumors might even fall short of the truth.

Given time to consider it, Darnell was a hell of a nice name for a man.

ELEVEN

A short stroll took Darnell past an office with the single word "Marshal" hand-painted on the window. The paint ran down from the letters like spindly spider legs, each ending in a little globbed foot on the bottom sill. He stepped inside the door into a stuffy room containing a single desk and two chairs. A wood stove stood in the corner. The occupant of one of the chairs stared at him across boots hoisted onto the desk. A brightly polished badge reflected light from the man's vest.

"Are you the marshal?"

The front legs of the tipped chair grated to the floor as the man rose and extended a hand. "I'm Bryce Cummings, deputy marshal. Morgan Courtney's the marshal. He should be along any minute now."

Darnell took the offered hand. "Darnell Baynes."

Cummings's eyes sharpened for a second, and then he laughed. "Heard of you, unless there's more than one by that name. You the one from Louisiana?"

"I'm one of them if there's more than one."

"Grab one of those cups and pour yourself

some coffee." Cummings gestured toward the coffeepot on top of the stove. Four tin cups hung from a line of nails in the wall behind the pot. He dropped back into his chair, tipped it back, and lifted his boots to the scarred desk top. Showing a fine sense of balance on the tilted chair, he stretched an arm to open a drawer and pulled out a two-inch stack of posters. He shuffled the posters into an orderly pile in his lap and started through them.

Darnell poured coffee and took the other chair.

The silence between them didn't seem to bother the deputy, and Darnell didn't want to show impatience, so he awaited the man's pleasure. After a few minutes, finished with the posters, Cummings slapped them back into the drawer and slammed it shut. He glanced at Darnell. "Sometimes Morgan sticks those things in the drawer without telling me when new ones come in."

Darnell blew on the steaming coffee. "I'm not wanted."

"No offense intended. We draw wanted men out in these parts, get thick as flies. Good climate. Lots of room. Pays a public servant to check who's in the neighborhood."

"Commendable. Rough job?"

Cummings smiled. "Pays good. I might be able to help you, Baynes, if you don't want to wait for Morgan. I'm his night man."

"I own part of the Raymond and Ely. One of our stockholders got shot in the back recently, man named Fitzpatrick. Any luck finding out who did it?"

Cummings shrugged. "Happened on my shift. One shot. Heard it myself. Square in the back. Close. Burned his coat. Sometimes a single shot like that sounds mighty final. Know what I mean?"

Darnell nodded and lifted a palm in agreement, the gesture of one man of the world to another.

"I found him about two minutes later. No witnesses. Nothing to go on. Nobody bragged about it. Sometimes we find out who did a killing the next time the killer has a few drinks. Most of the time there's no question who did it anyhow. We usually don't even have to go to court."

"Oh?"

"Man does a killing, he runs, vanishes like a raindrop in the desert, but some of these boys would rather shoot it out than stand trial or go to jail. Morgan handles them just fine. We went three weeks last month burying two a week. Morgan's not a patient man. Had a couple of saloon keepers in here griping."

"What was the gripe?"

"Morgan just leaves them where they fall. The saloon has to clean up, pay for the burying. They figured they were getting more than their share. After they hollered and stomped around awhile, Morgan said, 'Thank you. Always glad to hear from citizens,' and went back to reading the paper. They went on back to pissing in their whiskey or whatever they do to it."

"I see."

Cummings dropped his feet to the floor and leaned elbows on the desk.

"You own part of one of the two biggest mines around here, but you don't act like you know what's going on."

"I just got in from California yesterday."

"Yeah, we get a lot of high fliers drifting through from there. Selling stock in holes in the ground is big business. Lots of difference between a hole in the ground and a silver mine, Baynes. You look around while you're here. There's holes everywhere. They sell stock, draw big salaries, pay for a hundred miners but only hire five, move some rock, and then quit soon as the money's gone. They say how sorry they are to those who bought in, and then they start selling stock in another hole."

Darnell nodded. Nothing new about this.

Cummings went on. "Other than the Raymond and Ely, you got the Washington and Creole. That's about it for the real big ones, but there's about twenty others making fairly hefty money. Then there's about twenty more two-bit outfits digging enough ore to pay wages and talk big. Tom and Frank Newlands, owners of the Washington and Creole, claim you boys are mining their ore. They claim the whole mountain. You know that?"

Darnell nodded again slowly, but this he had not heard. Ownership became a shaky and fragile concept when the whole state hierarchy reeked with corruption. The state of Nevada owned the undisputed championship for venal conduct. The legislature, law officers, and judges admired and appreciated the highest bidder for their favors.

Nevada citizens fought for jury duty, a chance to make a nice bonus for soft work. Darnell had even heard one story about a jury, locked up in the courthouse second story, lowering a boot on a string to collect their just due. The boot had been lowered twice, a crude but effective sealed bid system for the two sides in the dispute.

The balance sheet for the Raymond and Ely showed enormous expenditures for legal fees. He and Thackery accepted that "legal fees" was a term that covered bribes as well. A businessman did what he had to do, but that book entry was an open door for embezzlement too.

"You don't expect to find the man who shot Fitzpatrick?"

Cummings shook his head. "No telling. He's just one of ten or twenty unsolved murders that I know about. Not anything we can do unless somebody talks. Friend of yours, was he?"

"Didn't know him. Just curious."

Cummings looked up when a well-dressed man stepped through the door. Darnell's first impression came from a flash of spotless white linen. This man evidently gave a lot of business to the local Chinese laundry.

The chair legs hit the floor again as Cummings

came to his feet. "Morgan, meet Darnell Baynes. Baynes, this is Marshal Morgan Courtney."

"Pleased to meet you, Mr. Baynes." Courtney's expression gave no hint that the Baynes name struck a chord. He shook hands briefly and took the chair Cummings had vacated.

"My pleasure."

Talking while he moved, Cummings walked to the pot, poured a cup for Courtney, and placed it on the desk in front of him. "Mr. Baynes asked about the Fitzpatrick killing, Marshal. He's a stockholder in the Raymond and Ely like Fitzpatrick was."

Courtney nodded without comment and, it seemed, without interest.

Darnell, still on his feet after the swift handshake with the marshal, said, "I thought you ought to know Fitzpatrick's sister came in yesterday about the same time I did. After what happened to her brother, I thought you might want to keep an eye on her. It'd be a shame if something happened to her too."

Courtney leveled his gaze at Darnell. "We have seventy-five saloons, two hotels worthy of the name, thirty-five sporting houses, and about forty canvas flophouses. We get every tinhorn, con man, cardsharp, horse thief, rustler, gun slick and painted lady in the country drifting through this town. We got Irish trash that hasn't been sober or had a bath in ten years."

Courtney paused to take a breath and flick at a speck on his coat. Darnell had a moment to muse on the man's Irish accent before he continued. "We got a Chinese opium den right down the street. You expect me to look after a lone woman? I have two deputies in a town of five thousand that never sleeps. Keep her off the street at night and get her out of here as quick as you can. Otherwise, if you're concerned, walk behind her with your gun in your hand."

He turned to Cummings. "Anything happen last night I need to know about?"

"Quiet night. Half a dozen drunks got rolled. Half a dozen fistfights. One knife fight over to Carolyn's. An ore wagon rolled over a drunk."

"Kill him?"

"Lord yes."

"Driver do it on purpose?"

"Which one? Nobody saw it. A bunch of men hollered for me when they found the body. Wheel marks dead center. Didn't take an Indian tracker to figure it out. Busted a bottle he had in his coat. Couple of bystanders broke down and cried about that."

"Good job, Bryce. I'm going to breakfast. Nice to meet you, Baynes." Courtney walked to the door without tasting his coffee, a departing handshake, or even a glance at Darnell. He stopped beside the door to conduct a thorough scrutiny up and down the street before he stepped out.

Cummings didn't miss a beat. He seated himself again in Courtney's chair and picked up the tin cup.

Darnell said mildly, "Seemed in a hurry, didn't he?"

"Grumpy some mornings. I'm off duty soon's he gets a bite to eat. Anything else, Mr. Baynes?"

Darnell touched the brim of his hat in a parting salute and walked out. Morgan Courtney qualified as one of the most arrogant sons he'd met in years. A fastidious man, he'd been careful not to touch the dusty desk with hand or sleeve.

He considered exploring on foot, but since he needed to go by the livery to check on his horses anyway he decided to mount up. Both animals looked rested and alert but still showed too much rib. A few more days' rest would cure that. Meanwhile, a slow little tour wouldn't hurt his saddle horse. Besides, Darnell thought horses went a little crazy if kept stalled too much.

Pioche held no surprises for a man used to raw mining towns. Aside from mining, the major business interests always centered on extracting money from the miners. Men who worked long hours deep underground in dark, foul, dangerous conditions made good money. Mine foremen sought the strongest and toughest they could hire.

Peaceful, thoughtful workers could get on if they could swing a pick ten hours a day along with the toughs, and many could. Even so, men separated from families, subjected to grueling hard labor, and obliged to live in conditions unfit for farm animals soon built a head of steam. A few drinks and an occasional roll with a crib girl helped to keep the boiler from cracking, but blasts to relieve the monotony came frequently.

A careless word or an accidental jostle at a bar could start a head-busting riot. Men from rival mines sometimes took up sides with their employers like feuding families. The circling vultures, every kind of crooked freeloader born to mankind, gathered to prey on the naive and the drunk. The victims sometimes showed fangs of their own, so the predators joined the pushovers in boot hill.

Darnell kept his mount at a walk, pulling well to the side to escape the dust from twenty-mule-team ore wagons heading south. He remembered Raymond mentioning at supper last night an integrated mill at Bullionville, twenty miles south. An integrated mill accepted ore from several mines, usually charging a flat rate per ton of ore processed. At a flat rate, the mill had no particular incentive to extract the highest possible return from the ore. That might be where profits leaked from the till. He'd look into that as soon as time permitted.

He reined to a halt beside a building under construction. The frame stood starkly exposed with its raw, green timbers that had never seen a drying kiln. Stone walls two feet thick were rising around the frame. One of the masons walked over to a nearby water barrel and nodded pleasantly to Darnell. "Howdy."

Darnell gestured to the work site. "What's it going to be?"

"Jail. Going to be a beauty."

"Looks like good work." Darnell touched his hat and rode on, smiling to himself. The birth of civic pride came in many forms. After all, no citizen would want to brag about living in a town with a flimsy jail. When completed, this one looked like it would be stout enough to resist an attack with cannons. No reason at all for the jail not to be the finest building in town. Local citizens always knew what they needed most.

He rode past the Chinatown with the Chinese laundry shacks and eateries he had known would be located somewhere in town, pigtailed workers busy with their endless drive. Every mining town had one. Spotless Marshal Courtney almost had to be their best individual laundry customer. Darnell placed a bet with himself that the marshal never paid a dime. Taxes came in many guises. The hotel, with its surprisingly clean tablecloths, napkins, and bug-free bed linens, probably offered the largest business account.

Darnell watched the busy traffic. Pioche had nothing but ore. Water, wood, food, and everything else came through the dust on wagons. He remembered John Ely the night before volunteering to Miss Fitzpatrick the origin of the town's moniker. It came from the name of a Frenchman, an early arrival in the area, probably pronounced "Pie-oh-shay" originally, but the name fell off the tongue of miners as "Pee-oh-tch."

The sun stood high in the sky, and Darnell thought lunch might come in handy. He turned toward the hotel and kicked his horse into a lope. Maybe the Amazon would be there. She might attack him. That woman surely had a knot in her tail. Darnell chuckled to himself and pulled his hat down like a man riding toward rough winds. He'd just have to fight her off as best he could, and keep an eye peeled for the nearest door or window. Anybody who planned to meet hostiles without looking for escape routes had lost his thinking cap.

The Amazon sat with Raymond at the same table she'd claimed at breakfast. She spoke a quick word or two to him, and Raymond turned immediately to wave at Darnell and gesture to an empty chair at their table. Darnell hung his hat on the empty hall tree beside the door, nodded a wordless greeting to the Amazon, and took a seat. A swift glance around told him he was the only man in the room who'd removed his hat.

Raymond said, "Miss Fitzpatrick just asked me to explain how ore is freighted to Bullionville. She says she isn't satisfied with our records."

"What's the problem?" Darnell hated to talk business at meals. A man needed some relief once in a while, but he decided not to make an issue of his preferences. The Amazon knew his feelings about the matter. He'd made them plain at breakfast, but that would mean little or nothing to her. In any event, no food had been brought to them yet. He looked around for the waiter.

Raymond saw Darnell's searching glance and spoke quickly. "We saw you tie your horse in front, Mr. Baynes, so we went ahead and ordered for you. No choice. We eat what they cooked today, whatever it is."

Darnell nodded and said, "Thanks."

The Amazon spoke in the flat, quietly emphatic tone now familiar to Darnell. "You asked what the problem is, Mr. Baynes. It seems a simple matter to me. The bookkeeper knows how many wagons of ore leave the mine. He pays the freight by the trip. But he has no record of how many loads of ore arrive at the mill. The mill charges us by the ton, not the wagon load. We have no way to cross-check to see if every wagon loaded with our ore gets delivered to the mill."

"Where the devil else would it go, Miss Fitzpatrick?" Raymond sounded mildly amused, and Darnell shot him a quick glance. Raymond might not pass the noon hour with his head still intact unless he changed his tune. She must have spent the morning at the mine headquarters, and she must have a trained eye to interpret records and fish up this kind of question so quickly.

She responded exactly as Darnell expected. "I have no idea where it might go, Mr. Raymond. I can only tell you that proper supervision requires accounting for every load."

Raymond's jaw muscles bulged. He took a long, slow breath. He had just been accused of inferior supervision, and he knew it, but he couldn't quite believe it yet.

Relentless, she pressed on. "You have no representative at the mill?"

"We don't want a man hanging around down there with his pants full of money to pay people, Miss Fitzpatrick. We pay independent freighters who own their own wagons right here at headquarters. We got a safe here and armed guards. They deliver and come back for the next load, and we pay them when they get back. Perlman and Perlman's freight gets paid once a week. They send over a rep for their money."

The Amazon asked, eyes fixed on Raymond, "What's to stop a freighter from saying Washington and Creole instead of Raymond and Ely when mill hands ask which mine the ore came from?" She sat waiting for an answer. When none came, she asked, "Who'd know the difference down there? Who'd care?"

"They know our freighters."

"Does this Perlman company always send the same drivers?" Again she got no answer. "The independents never haul for anybody else?" No answer. "Would a couple of dollars in his pocket make a man forget which mine he came from?"

Raymond nodded. "I think I'd better look

into this." He forced a short laugh. "My bookkeeper won't like the extra work."

Without inflection, the Amazon said, "Fire him. Hire a better man. The mill charges us by the ton. That means they weigh each wagon load, I presume?"

Raymond replied, "They have a big scale."

"That means they could note who the driver is for each load and the date. We'd have the same record back here. Occasionally, we could send a man down there and compare records. If they didn't match, we'd have names of drivers who shouldn't work for us anymore."

Raymond said slowly, "I don't see why that wouldn't work."

She unfolded her napkin and looked at the food the waiter had placed in front of her. "Isn't it nice we finished talking about commerce in time. Mr. Baynes hates to talk business when he's eating."

TWELVE

The meal finished, Raymond excused himself, and Darnell rose to do the same. He ducked his head in a wordless bow, but before he could turn away, her upraised hand stopped him.

"I wonder if you could help me, Mr. Baynes?"

"I'm at your service." He leaned one hand on the back of his chair.

"I have my saddle with me, but Mr. Raymond said he knew of no horses around here that were accustomed to a sidesaddle. He said he didn't want the responsibility of finding a mount for me since he doesn't consider himself an expert about horses."

"You consider me better qualified?"

"Perhaps unfairly. I've heard you trained horses years ago and your youngest son has built a reputation in that business. Is that just part of the reputation you deny?"

The Amazon had a way of looking at a man. Her stare seemed to dare him, seemed to imply she didn't expect much and that if he couldn't produce results he would only confirm her low opinion. Darnell thought for a moment, not tempted to speak quickly. The easy way out of this would be to apologize and follow Raymond's lead, duck the responsibility. To rise to the challenge in her expression didn't appeal to him one bit. Men who responded to that kind of testing hadn't outgrown boyish desires to show off.

On the other hand, he could provide a mount for her with no effort at all. Why not offer a small favor? It'd give his pack horse a chance to get out of the confinement of a stall for light exercise once in a while. Do a favor and draw benefit from it. Not a bad deal. She could, possibly, be the kind who remembered favors.

His pack horse, a calm, gentle mare with good blood, was a gift from Ward. His youngest son could train a horse to serve tea and crumpets if he put his mind to it. The diffident Ward had said, "Nice horse for a lady, if you find one who'll ride with you, Pa."

Ward never made such comments lightly. Darnell had taken the remark as simply another broad hint from one of his sons that they wouldn't mind seeing their father enjoy female company once in a while. All of them made sly hints of that kind. In fact, in recent years, his sons had been more often blunt than sly. But if Ward said a horse would be good for a lady to ride, a prudent man had better listen and remember. The boy never joked or made careless talk about horses.

"I may have a suitable animal myself, Miss Fitzpatrick. We could put your saddle on my mare, put you up on her, and walk her around inside the corral to see how she behaves."

"Wonderful. You thought about it so long I thought you were coming up with a way to say no. A nice little mare, that will be marvelous."

Darnell cleared his throat softly. "No, ma'am, not a nice little mare, I'm afraid. This is a long-legged, hot-blooded animal who loves to run, but she has a gentle nature, and she's had training from the best horseman I know."

"From your son, I suppose?"

"Yes, ma'am." He grinned into her unblinking stare. Ward was the best. That was the straight truth. She could swallow that or choke, her choice.

She aimed a smile at him so warm and friendly he almost took a step back in surprise. The Amazon's appearance changed so suddenly he caught his breath.

Her matter-of-fact tone hadn't changed, though. She said flatly, "The only time I find vanity pleasing in a man is when he speaks proudly of his family. You really admire your son, don't you?"

"Sons, ma'am. I have three." Darnell still felt a little off balance, so he thought he'd better change the subject. That smile had come so unexpectedly, had melted an icy impression in an instant, leaving him groping for a new way to deal with this woman. Lots of otherwise clever men had turned foolish trying to win smiles from females much less impressive than this one. "I'm surprised Mr. Raymond couldn't have been more helpful."

"I think my manner upsets him."

Clever, damnably clever. Her comment carried an implied compliment for Darnell and the reverse for Raymond. She might as well, if she weren't so canny, have said, "You are not upset by confident, competent women like he is. You are too smart for that."

A surge of caution welled up so strongly in him that he stiffened, a foolish reflex. A man needed to keep careful watch or he'd find himself manipulated by this woman and liking it. She seemed to be the type of quarrelsome woman who either manipulated or maimed, with nothing in between.

He spoke slowly, as if he'd taken time to ponder her comment about Raymond, and deliberately twisted her meaning. "Yes, ma'am. I think you could upset a man if you took a notion." Full of surprises, she showed color. By heaven, she blushed like a regular female and looked away. Unpredictable as damp powder. No telling from one minute to the next whether she'd fire, fizzle, or fail to burn at all.

"Would you mind if we tried the horse right now? I'm used to riding almost every day, and I've missed it terribly."

"I'm at your service, ma'am."

"I need to change and get my saddle. I'll be right back."

She rose and walked away, leaving him with a hand lifted too late to stop her. If she saw the gesture, she ignored it. He wanted to offer to carry her saddle down the stairs for her, but chasing her to her room might not be prudent, might cause talk. He let the hand drop, snagged his hat, and walked out to a bench on the front porch. No wonder her trunk weighed a ton. She'd even brought a saddle in it.

He sat down and stifled a yawn. Darnell Baynes knew he was neither drowsy nor bored. He yawned when his nerves tightened. Other men scratched, trembled, needed to make water. Darnell yawned, and it angered him to find himself wound up tight.

He'd ridden many hard miles to get to this forsaken rock pile of a town, only to spend his first afternoon bathing and barbering like a fop for her benefit. Now she'd hooked him into spending the next afternoon escorting her on a pleasure ride. And he looked forward to it like a dry pasture waiting for rain. Oh well, he'd not started out in a hurry to do business. No need to get himself stirred up and in a big hurry now.

No call to sit here like a simpleton either. He jumped to his feet, mounted, and rode to the livery. The mare nuzzled him when he flipped her blanket across her back and let her out of the stall. "You better behave yourself, girl," he muttered. "You throw that Amazon and she'll jump up and whip us both." He mounted again and led the mare back to the hotel.

He imagined himself telling Thackery about this when he got back to Sacramento. "I thought it vital to establish a good association with this woman when I found out she was a big stockholder. I moved on that right away. Felt it was absolutely necessary." No need to tell Thackery she buckled his knees with a smile. He didn't need to know everything.

She came out lugging her saddle. No effort. Strong woman. Carried it like she took it with her everywhere. Darnell grabbed it without asking, and she released it with another smile. One side of her coat pulled away from her body for a blink of time before it fell back into place. That was all the view he got, but he had a quick and sharp eye.

The warm flash of a brass housing with the curved butt turned forward showed from a leather holster tucked under the coat. Darnell had seen and admired the new Colt .41-caliber "house gun" in a shop in Sacramento. At the time, he hadn't thought it much of a hideout weapon, since it looked bigger and more powerful than most, with a four-shot cylinder if he remembered correctly. But her stylish riding coat, once she had it primly buttoned, hid the weapon perfectly. He had never seen a woman wear a shoulder holster before.

He slapped the Amazon's saddle on the mare. "I don't think we need a corral. We'll try walking her right here in the street. If she's going to act up, we'll know right away."

Darnell handed the Amazon up to the saddle and grabbed the reins. The mare didn't even roll her eyes, and Darnell laughed.

"What's so funny?"

He handed her the reins and stepped into his saddle. "Miss Fitzpatrick, my son told me this horse was fine for a lady to ride. I had a laugh on myself for questioning something *he* said about a horse. Then I had another thought — I remembered how he trains horses for ladies. That boy leaves nothing to chance."

"He does something you find amusing?"

"Yes, ma'am. Ward puts on a skirt and rides a sidesaddle."

She laughed, a delighted sound, charming to hear. "That must be a sight. Why?"

"He says horses hate surprises. A woman's skirt caught in the wind might scare anybody who's never seen it before. He carries a blanket too, flops it all around, makes high-pitched screams and giggles, does all kinds of crazy things."

She reined her horse close to his and aimed a broad smile at him. "Ward must have known some very flighty women who shouldn't be allowed near a horse."

Ward. She'd said Ward. Darnell racked his brain trying to remember if he'd mentioned Ward's name to her. He didn't think so. The Amazon had been listening to somebody and committing a lot of things about him to memory. Probably didn't mean anything. Lots of people knew the names of the outlaw Baynes clan. People had asked about his sons by name many times before, people he'd never met in his life.

Darnell found his mouth dry, and he searched

out a cigar from his coat. He rolled it around in his mouth and left it unlit. If the Amazon pulled that Colt on him, he didn't know what he'd do. He'd already made up his mind not to turn his back on her. Now he realized that wouldn't make any difference if she decided to take a shot at him unless he was ready to pull his own Navy to defend himself. The Colt house gun wouldn't have much range, but nobody rode with a lady and stayed a safe hundred feet or so away. Nor could he ride close enough to try to knock it away. That wouldn't work. He'd need arms five or six feet long.

He couldn't sit still and let her shoot him. Could he shoot a woman? Never gave it a thought. Didn't like the idea. Besides, if she pulled that Colt and he shot her, he'd have to ride to South America to be safe from a rope. *Ride* — that was his only chance. If she pulled iron, he'd ride like the devil pursued him and hope she missed, the Colt misfired, or she hit him in a spot he could tolerate and survive.

If she only got one clean shot, he might live through this ride. At a gallop, with him ducking and dodging, she might empty that popgun and never hit him again. Nothing came to him about how he could prevent her from getting a good, clean first shot. Not being able to shoot back at somebody was pure awful, made a man's stomach wad up in a knot. Worst tight spot in the world. Couldn't do anything. Couldn't even throw rocks.

Once the ugly thought came to him that she might be dangerous, Darnell found nothing to do but hide in a fatalistic mood. It took less than five minutes for his critical eye to tell him she rode like a Valkyrie, those mythical beautiful maidens chosen to escort dead heroes to paradise. Seat firm, back straight, head high, showing such confidence she seemed to pay no attention to the horse, the Amazon looked born to the saddle. She didn't wait for him to lead; she just put her mare to a lope and headed for the open desert.

He groaned inside. He'd have a hell of a time riding away from her. No chance, unless lightning struck her from a clear blue sky. He'd put her on a superbly trained horse as good as any to be found in Nevada. She and the mare raced through the sunshine like one creature, a magnificent thing to watch. If it had to happen this way, at least this was a beautiful day to die. Darnell yawned so hard his eyes watered.

The Amazon eased to a trot and down to a walk, letting him overtake without looking back for him. When he came alongside, she said, "What's her name?"

"Flea."

Another musical burst of laughter. "No, really, what do you call her?"

"Flea. Ward said she's nimble, sure-footed. Nice and tall too. He says she's a good jumper."

"She's the best I've ridden in years. Why is she so thin?"

All right, so she had a good eye for horses. He caught a sting in the comment. What the devil, he didn't starve his animals. "Came all the way from California with me. Carson Pass was no picnic. Long, hard ride. Not rested yet. We just got here yesterday, same as you."

"Did you find out anything this morning?" She turned black eyes on him, direct as gun barrels.

"About what?"

She pulled the mare to a stop. "Darnell, I'm tired of sparring with you. I always lose. You win, but why bother? Doesn't anything matter to you? Don't you care about anything?"

"I care about things. I care about riding with a lady with a gun hidden under her coat, a lady who doesn't seem to like me taking me out of sight into an empty desert."

She unbuttoned her coat and drew the Colt. It took all he had, but he faced her without flinching. The sun warm on his face, he regretted he'd not taken time to write a note to his sons. They'd never dream to look for a woman, and they'd surely come searching for his killer. He should have delayed. He could have put her off until tomorrow. That would have given him time to do one last thing for his boys, a simple little note of farewell, and it wouldn't have taken much quick thinking.

A man should say good-bye to his kin, given a chance, and he'd missed his. So many things came to mind he'd like to say to his boys, but no man ever got all he wanted done in one lifetime. Every life ended too soon.

Darnell looked her straight in the eye when her arm came up. Her gaze never wavered. In spite of his best effort, he felt his whole body tighten, waiting for the jolt. He knew his breath would whistle like a winded mule, so he closed his dry throat and held it.

At that instant the decision came to him. If this black-eyed woman shot him, he'd go for her, pull her down with him, and wring her neck. Pride comes before a fall, but he knew he could do it. Over two hundred pounds of muscle and bone, he wouldn't die too quick to get it done. She dragged out the tension with the cool efficiency of an Apache waving a skinning knife in front of a captive, testing the enemy's courage.

Finally, she said impatiently, "Go ahead. Take it."

He looked down. The butt of her Colt faced him.

"I don't think I need it if I'm with you. You can carry it if it makes you feel better."

Darnell had never fainted in his life, but he knew he neared the edge, and he had no idea what to do about it. He took a deep breath and fought down the shakes, near weak enough to topple from the saddle. He didn't want to speak, but he felt forced to reply. He couldn't sit gulping like a squashed toad. By some miracle, his voice came out without a quaver.

"No thank you, ma'am, but if you don't mind, I'd like to get down. I'd just like to sit on the ground for a minute." Without waiting for her answer, he stepped out of the saddle and sank down on his heels. He sat with shoulders forward and head bowed to hide his face under the brim of his hat. He thought he might try to light his cigar as soon as he felt sure he could handle a match.

Her boots thumped when she dropped from the saddle and made slow gritty crunches until her shadow fell across him. His hat lifted, and he found her kneeling, face only inches from his, his hat in her hand. "What on earth made you think that?"

"What?"

"Don't you dare dodge me, Darnell. I won't have it." She slapped him with his own hat. The crushed cigar fell to the ground.

He lifted both hands to protect his stinging face. "Seemed you took a strong dislike for me. I figured maybe you took me for your brother's killer."

"I'll never joke about you being tough again. How could you do a thing like that? How could any human being just sit and wait to be shot? I never dreamed what you were thinking until the last moment, and then I couldn't believe my eyes."

"Stupid. I got caught. Too dumb to run. Too dumb to shoot back. Ran plumb out of ideas. Never had a woman pull a gun on me before."

She stared at him, black eyes never seeming to blink. “Too proud to run. Too much a gentleman to shoot a woman. Most of all, stupid. You’re an imbecile.”

“Thank you.” Darnell got a glimpse of his Stetson coming around at him again. He stuck out a hand and snagged it just in time. “That’s a tiresome habit. I wish you wouldn’t be hitting on me. It’s sweet of you, but I get sparked, and we only met yesterday.”

She gave up his hat after a brief struggle. “Your offhand manner is outrageous. If you must, I’ll tolerate it around other people. You seem to think it’s clever. When we ride together every day we shall have privacy, and I see no reason you should keep up a silly pretense.”

“We’re going to ride every day, are we?”

She nodded. “We have no other way to talk with perfect assurance we won’t be overheard. To whisper together in the hotel dining room would start rumors. It would look like romantic nonsense.”

“Nonsense? Thank you again. Remarks like that make a man feel chesty. What does riding around together every day look like anyhow? What if somebody asks to come along, and we say no? What’ll that look like?”

“We’ll have to risk it. Besides, I love to ride. It’s the only way I can keep from feeling like a prisoner trapped inside stuffy rooms all the time.”

Darnell came to his feet, and she stood with him. Pleased that his knees felt strong under him, he looked down at her. "You're big enough for romance, seems to me."

She made a sour mouth and raised a hand to her eyes. "I like you better seated. I don't have to look up and get the sun in my eyes."

He sat down again, and she knelt beside him. Darnell scanned the empty ground around them, edgy about how this woman held too much of his attention. A rattler could cross his boot and he might not notice. "Now you're the one dodging. I said you're perfect for a romance with me. You're halfway presentable if a man likes Amazons, and I'm handsome as the devil's deputy and big enough to fight you off if you get too randy. Romance gives us an excuse. Other people might not catch on we're really talking business. Matter of fact, maybe we won't be except now and then. Why fake a courtship? Real is always better than fake."

"That's impossible for me."

He deliberately scanned her from head to foot, noticing with satisfaction the color that came to her face while he held on to the guarded expression he used when examining a horse he might buy. Didn't pay to show approval if it might raise the price. He kept his voice flat, businesslike. "Don't see why. Must be something that doesn't show. If I can't see it, nobody else will."

"It always dies on the vine. It's best avoided. I'm not interested."

He punched his Stetson back into shape and

left it hanging from one hand while he sat on his heels squinting into the distance. After allowing the silence to stretch for a moment or two, he used a dry tone. "Three mighty good reasons." He waited several seconds like he was thinking it through some more before he added, "All right, bossy women gather dust on the shelf. Not much market for them. We can fake it."

"You can't even make an agreement without some kind of little barb, some petty slight, can you?"

"Just trying to stay even, ma'am."

THIRTEEN

By the time he dropped the Amazon off at the hotel, put Flea back in her stall and paid a little extra attention to her, and climbed back into the saddle again, the sun had drifted past a mid-afternoon bearing. He still had hours of daylight left.

Darnell figured he'd circled and coasted long enough. He rode straight to the Raymond and Ely. The first employee he ran into when he approached the headquarters building lifted a rifle and shouted, "Stop right there."

When Darnell reined to a halt, the guard walked closer and spoke politely. "You're on private property, sir. No trespassing is allowed."

"I'm Darnell Baynes. I'm a stockholder."

The guard lowered his rifle at once. "Welcome, Mr. Baynes. Mr. Raymond told us to watch out for you. He's in the building straight ahead. Follow me, sir." He turned on his heel and walked straight to the ramshackle building. As soon as they arrived and Darnell swung down, the guard said, "Go right in, sir. Mr. Raymond is expecting you."

Darnell said, "Thank you. You've been most kind." As he watched the guard walk away without a backward glance, he congratulated whoever hired Raymond and Ely guards. If they were all like that one, crisp, courteous, alert, and carrying a rifle as if born with it in hand, their prior military service stood out as plain as a warning flag. Even so, that was probably a man picked and rehearsed to make a good show. Raymond seemed far too clever to miss a chance to impress a stockholder. No, John Ely was the showman. He probably took care of putting up a front.

When he stepped inside the open door, Raymond came from an adjoining room and said, "This way, Mr. Baynes. Just happened to look through the window and see you coming. Come in my office and have a seat. You might be able to help."

Darnell took a seat and watched Raymond circle his desk, grab a cigar box, and offer a cigar before dropping into his own chair. Darnell accepted with a derisive inner grin, remembering the last one he'd tried, now lying smashed somewhere out in the desert where the Amazon had slapped it out of his mouth. "I'm here to help if I can. What's the difficulty?"

"First, may I review a few things with you, just so we both know you're up-to-date?"

Darnell relaxed in his chair. The shrewd little miner's choice of words sounded smooth and routine, but his voice vibrated with tension, tight as a banjo string. "Please do, Mr. Raymond. I'd be obliged."

Raymond flattened his hands on the desk. "Thank you. As you probably know, the Washington and Creole operates right next to us. We take ore from the same mountain. Recently the owners, Tom and Frank Newlands, made us an offer. They've been fighting us in court for months, trying to make out that they own the whole mountain. Well, their ore has been running thin lately. They wanted to run a tunnel down to a lower level, hoping to find richer ore. It would take a huge effort to do it from their side, terribly expensive, so they asked if they could open a tunnel leading through our property. We're already mining at that level, so putting their tunnel through won't amount to half as much work."

When he stopped to take a breath, Darnell asked, "What did they offer?"

Raymond lifted a finger and nodded. "The right question, sir. They offered to withdraw their suit in the state court and not to renew their foolish effort to grab our claim by perverting the law. That's not the way they put it, but that's the way I describe it."

"And that would save us a railcar load of legal fees and bribes."

Raymond's face lost a little tension. "I appreciate your quickness, sir. That seemed a deal advantageous to everybody, so we agreed."

" 'We' being you and John Ely?"

"Correct, but John doesn't do much of this kind of thing. This is my end. He does most of our public relations, works with stockholders, does the hand-holding, talks to the newspapers, and all of that."

"He's not holding my hand. You are."

Raymond ventured a tight smile. "John's off to the state capital right now. Spends a lot of time up there. Things can get out of control in Nevada very quickly if one isn't on the scene up there to keep watch."

"And pay the right people."

"Right again. Anyway, the Newlandses sank their shaft through our property. Today one of our supervisors went down there to check their progress and found himself looking at tons of rich ore. They ran into ore on our property, so they stopped tunneling and started mining. Our supervisor said it looks like they've been taking our ore for a couple of weeks or so."

Darnell leaned forward to knock the ash from his cigar into a bowl on the desk. "So now you're planning your next move."

Raymond lifted a hand to signal he had more to say. "I sent a bunch of our guards over there to run them off. By the time my men got there, those damned Newlandses had barricaded the entrance. They've posted a dozen men with rifles, and they fired warning shots. Our men backed off fast, I'll tell you. We try not to hire complete idiots. It would be suicide to try to get in there now."

"The law?"

Raymond pulled the back of his hand across

his mouth and glanced at the door and out the window. He motioned to Darnell to draw him closer and lowered his voice. "Mr. Baynes, someone once said the law is an ass. He was wrong. The law is a hired killer. Morgan Courtney's real name is Richard Moriarty. Some time back he shot through a window and killed a man named O'Toole up in Virginia City after a trivial argument in a bar. He dropped out of sight for a while and showed up here in Pioche as a dandy with a new name along with his white linen suits and pick-pointed boots. We'd have never known except somebody from up there who knew him drifted through and recognized him in spite of his fancy new finery. They dragged him off to Virginia City for trial, but it came to nothing. The only witnesses had moved away and nobody could find them."

Darnell shrugged. "We don't need a good lawman with a gun. We need a lawman good with a gun."

Raymond glanced out the window and at the door again. "Need one or not, that's what we've got. I've lost count of how many men he's killed in Pioche. His kind of lawman thinks prisoners are inconvenient. His kind of lawman is also the most expensive kind. I sent for him a couple of hours ago. He's slow coming. That's the way he jacks up the price for doing his job. It might also mean that the Newlandses have already bought him off."

Darnell drew on his cigar and spoke through

the smoke. "That's why you keep looking out the window? You figure he's coming?"

Raymond slapped a hand on the desk several times, the outburst of a sorely tried, impatient man. "I keep hoping. If I have to go to him, that means the deal's dead. They've already bought him."

"Can't get it done with hired guns? You need him that bad?"

Raymond leaned forward again after another look out the window. "Look, Mr. Baynes, the man's a deadly, merciless killer. Everybody with a grain of sense is scared to death of him. He might be able to scare them off just because he's rightly earned his reputation. If not, by the book and God help us all, he's still the law. I have to consider appearances. Besides, if he takes their side, my men might end up facing murder charges after a fight just for defending my property."

Darnell nodded and pursed his lips. "All right. What's your bid to buy a badge? What do you plan to offer?"

For the first time, Raymond ventured a sour smile. "I plan to let him work my mine for a month. I'll buy the ore from him at a fair price based on what it assays."

"Why not offer him cash? At least you'd know the real cost up front."

"Cash in hand is worth more than ore in the ground, Mr. Baynes. I'm gambling Courtney won't know that."

Darnell tapped ash again. "All right. Offer one week. All my gambler friends say it's best to be ready for several raises."

"My plan exactly, and that bothers me. He'll be ready for that."

"Sure. It all depends on control. Can you control yourself?"

"What do you mean?"

"I once knew an amusing fellow, had perfect control of himself. He could pass wind whenever he took the notion. No telling when he might strike next. You need enough control to sweat on cue. If you can sweat enough when he raises the ante, you might get by with only two or three weeks, and he'll think he drove a hard bargain, put you to the wall. It might help if you can puke in the wastebasket before he leaves, just to make him feel nice and smug."

Raymond grinned, and Darnell felt better about him. The little miner must have needed someone to talk to who'd sympathize with the practical realities. His manner had changed. At first he'd acted like a man trying to show calm while an ore wagon rolled over his foot. Now he seemed more like a man keyed up for a good fight. Nothing like finding an understanding ally to raise a man's spirits.

Violent trouble erupting in his face while big stockholders looked down his throat could rattle anyone. No fighter likes to retreat to his corner and get hit some more by his handlers. The arrival of the Amazon predictably shook this tough little man badly. His type of man probably couldn't imagine that a woman might understand, might be helpful, might even be tougher than he. All he saw in her was a headstrong, unpredictable female liable to tip the scales against him at the most inopportune moment. Darnell felt a surge of sympathy. In Raymond's place, he'd most likely feel the same way.

"By heaven, Mr. Baynes, it looks like you brought me luck. Here he comes."

"I'm against the whole thing. I'll not support you in one bit of this."

"But I thought . . ."

"You thought right. Courtney doesn't need to know that. Best he thinks you have to fight for anything you offer him."

Raymond came to his feet and stuck a hand over the desk. Darnell stood and shook hands with him. When Raymond went to greet Courtney, Darnell pulled his chair back against the wall. His position away from the desk would add to the impression that he didn't want to be a part of the coming discussion.

The two men came in and, after casual greetings between Courtney and Darnell, took seats. After that, Darnell spoke not another word. The two men went straight to the point, spent no time on guarded language. Specific services called for specific language. Ten minutes later, Raymond and Courtney shook hands on the deal.

The only surprise came when Raymond pulled paper, pen, and ink from his desk and wrote down the agreement. Careful to keep a guarded expression, Darnell read the document when Raymond handed it to him. Neat. It looked like a simple rental agreement. Courtney, his deputies, and any allies he could muster would drive Washington and Creole men off the property for the right to work the Raymond and Ely rent-free for thirty consecutive days. Raymond further agreed to buy the ore from the renters for assay value.

Courtney turned to Darnell and said, "I hear you have quite a reputation, Mr. Baynes, but you haven't said a thing. I'm glad you didn't try to take the law into your own hands, but I could make you a deputy. Would you like to sign on?"

Straight-faced, Darnell said, "Thank you. Gun smoke makes me sneeze, and I don't like charging barricades, but I'd like to keep up with what's going on. This whole affair seems irregular at best, but Mr. Raymond has the power to make such arrangements over my objections. I have no choice but to go along."

Courtney put on a smug little smile. "I guess Mr. Raymond just wanted you here to be a witness to the deal. No need for that. I carry witnesses with me everywhere I go." His hand brushed over the holstered self-cocking Whistler pistol at his hip.

"You realize that Mr. Raymond has given away a whole month's production? That's almost equal to a ten-percent interest in the mine for a whole year." He managed to inject a wounded tone into the last statement.

"Better than to lose it all, don't you think, Mr. Baynes? I don't want to run at a bunch of rifles either. We'll have to try to sneak up on them at night or something. I need to go look at how they're fixed and get me some men to help."

"I'd be obliged if you'd include me in the planning. I might offer a few suggestions."

Courtney hesitated for a second, eyeing Darnell. Then he nodded. "We'll call you in soon as I see how things start to add up." He walked out.

Raymond stood leaning both fists on his desk. After Courtney had walked his horse out of sight, Darnell said softly, "Well done."

"This is a hell of a business. This is a hell of a state to do business in." Raymond gazed down at his desk and shook his head, shoulders slumped. "And that is one hell of a rotten, sorry Irishman."

Darnell smoothed his coat and straightened his Stetson. "Yeah, but it's been a heavenly day for a ride through the splendid desert scenery."

He could feel Raymond's astonished stare when he walked out and mounted. The little miner probably figured he had a major stockholder who'd lost his wits.

Darnell wondered what the Amazon would pull out of her witchcraft trunk to wear to the supper table tonight. Nice to think about a little thing like that on the eve of what was shaping up to be the ominous quiet before the start of a bloody shoot-out war. With hired guns blazing away at each other, the people who did the hiring couldn't expect to stand aside. In this kind of scuffle, the owners made the best targets.

FOURTEEN

The Amazon didn't disappoint. When Darnell strolled into the hotel dining room that evening, she sat at her usual table, dressed like she expected the Queen of England to drop by any minute. A thread of a gold chain around her neck supported a striking pendant, a ruby surrounded by diamonds. Her lustrous green dress had a high neck trimmed with white lace. Darnell took the dress to be silk, but he could never be sure about silk unless he laid a hand to it. The risk involved in that kind of test put a grin on him.

Two men sat at the table with her, both leaping forward as if in earnest conversation. She looked up and caught Darnell's eye. Instantly, her hand rose in a languid summons. Both her companions glanced around, saw Darnell coming, and looked as pleased as treed mountain lions.

"Good evening, Darnell. Please join us. I'd like to introduce you to these gentlemen." She gestured to the man on her left. "This is Mr. Tom Newlands." The indolent hand drifted vaguely toward the man on her right. "And this is Mr. Frank Newlands. They were kind enough to come by and introduce themselves, and I knew they'd want to meet you too. Gentlemen, this is Mr. Darnell Baynes."

Neither rose or offered a hand. Frank Newlands said, "We're talking business."

Darnell's grin widened at the tone. The man qualified as a perfect dunce if he thought he could dismiss someone the Amazon invited to her table. Darnell had an amazingly clear vision of what the poor fellow would look like trying to extract a dinner plate buried in his head. The vision brought a chuckle from him that caused the brothers to exchange puzzled glances. Darnell found himself enjoying their confusion. They had to wonder what kind of man laughed at an insolent snub.

Newlands's rebuff might just as well have been wind on the other side of the mountain to the smiling Amazon. "Please take a seat, Darnell." She turned the smile on the two grim-faced Newlandses and added, "I neglected to tell these gentlemen that we have an appointment for a private dinner, but I'm sure their business won't take much longer."

She'd called him by his first name twice in about ten seconds and plainly told them they were running out of welcome. The signal couldn't be missed unless these men were pigheaded. Darnell sat down, lifted his napkin with his left hand, leaned toward the Amazon, and said, "A striking gem, Linda. A genuine pigeon's-blood oriental ruby, I believe, surely from Upper Burma near Moguk. Note the color, gentlemen. It's clearly not one of those inferior spinel rubies. I don't believe I've ever seen you wear it before, my dear. A recent gift?"

By the time he finished that line of prattle, with the Newlandses unable to resist the pleasant opportunity to inspect the Amazon's imposing bust, Darnell, hiding his move behind the unfolding napkin, had seated himself comfortably with his Navy in his right hand.

"No, it's been in the family a long time, but I don't wear it often." Her smile never varied. "These gentlemen own the Washington and Creole mine, Darnell. They were just telling me that we've invested in a worthless claim. They say we're mining ore that belongs to them."

Frank Newlands, corners of his mouth drawn down, asked, " 'Our' investment? You got money invested in the Raymond and Ely mine too, Baynes?"

Darnell nodded. "Yes, I do. I just came in from California to find out why our managers tolerate you. I don't think that can continue anymore."

"Tolerate us?" Frank Newlands's jaw tightened. Both he and his brother had square chins and hair the color of a rusted shovel. There the resemblance ended. Frank, although seated, was obviously taller than his brother and looked fifty pounds heavier, with jowls already becoming prominent and a hairline starting to retreat.

Tom appeared older and sported a splotched,

unhealthy pallor. When he smiled, the expression seemed oddly out of place on his face, like a tear in a soiled blanket. "You think you tolerate us?"

"Yes, seems unnecessary to me. I intended to confer with the major stockholders about making you an offer, more out of sympathy than anything else. But it would save us the minor legal expense involved in evicting you. However, this recent activity of yours seems so tacky, so immature, I don't know whether any of the stockholders will feel generous."

Darnell now felt sure the acerbic Tom was the older brother and the real decision maker of the two. When Tom entered the conversation, Frank fell silent. Tom Newlands now leaned forward, and Darnell thought of a blotched cobra taking its upright stance, preparing to strike.

"What makes you think we need you to be generous?"

Darnell laughed in his face. "You're so desperate you trick your way onto our claim with a sad story and an offer to stop making a nuisance of yourself in court. It's obvious your ore is wretched stuff, so you want to get to a deeper level hoping to find better color. Otherwise, why ask our generous permission to sink a shaft through our property? Then you get into our rich ore, and you stoop to outright theft. When the theft is discovered, you resort to hired thugs behind a barricade so you can try to steal some more. It's all a pitiful dance in a tattered costume, don't you think?"

Tom Newlands continued to lean forward, eyes fixed on Darnell. "I've heard of a Darnell Baynes, an outlaw supposed to have gone straight. You him?"

Darnell met his stare and smirked. "Who said I've gone straight? This is my kind of game. I just hate to see small-timers like you give outlawing a bad name. It's a fool's game to try to steal from a chief. It's too risky."

Newlands, eyes still locked with Darnell's, asked, "You making threats, big man?"

"Dumb question unless you're a little deaf."

Frank Newlands scraped his chair back and snarled, "We don't have to take your lip." He brushed his coat back from his hip.

Darnell said evenly, "Go ahead, Fat Frank, go for your gun." He cocked the Navy, the sound loud and clear in the suddenly quiet dining room. Without a sideward glance, Darnell knew the skittish Pioche citizens, at first sign of trouble such as this, had prepared themselves to dive for safety. "As soon as you do, I'll shoot your brother about four inches below his belt buckle. It's a tricky place for a man to get shot, don't you think, Tom? Getting a bullet there might change your attitude about all kinds of things."

Tom Newlands broke off the staring contest with Darnell. He turned his head very slowly to look at his brother. Frank licked lips gone dry and seemed to shrink. Tom said quietly, "Go outside and wait for me. Don't even look back until you get outside. Go clear out in the street and stay away from the windows." Frank turned without another word and walked out. As soon as his brother passed through the door, Tom Newlands asked, "You had that gun under there on me all this time?"

Darnell nodded. "I carry it for snakes."

The Amazon, still smiling like a pleasant hostess, said, "Good night, Mr. Newlands."

"Good night, Miss Fitzpatrick." His gaze came back to Darnell, and he waited until he got a small nod before he slowly came to his feet and walked out. As soon as he vanished, the buzz of conversation began again in the crowded room.

When Darnell glanced around, all the patrons in the dining room made a point to be looking another direction. He eased the Navy off cock, spun the cylinder under the table, counting the clicks so the hammer would rest again on the empty chamber, and slipped the weapon back into his holster.

The Amazon said placidly, "They offered to buy my stock for a tenth of its value. Didn't want to see a helpless woman lose everything."

"What did you say?"

"I said thank you but no. They didn't seem satisfied with my answer. That's when you came in."

"You ready to eat?"

"How can you be hungry so soon after something like that?"

"It's an ailment I've had a long time." He signaled the waiter who nodded but gestured toward another table. Darnell nodded back, accepting that the waiter would come as soon as he could get loose.

"Darnell?"

"Yeah?"

"You said they shouldn't try to steal from a chief. What did that mean?"

Darnell rubbed his mouth for a second. "Most every place has its own special language, and it doesn't change very fast. I rode through Nevada with my sons awhile back. When we came through, folks here called an important man a chief. Almost always a chief around here is a man with several killings to his credit, either hired out or done personally. Messing with a chief is only fun for the kind of men who like to poke short sticks at rattlers."

"Do you?"

"Poke short sticks at rattlers? No, ma'am, not even long sticks. They don't like it."

"Never mind snakes. Do you have several killings to your credit?"

"Oh, that. It's not the kind of thing a man should bluff about."

"You sat right in front of me and threatened to kill them? Is that what all that meant?"

"Yes, ma'am. Don't put on a horrified act. You knew. Don't sit there and pretend you didn't."

"Would you really have shot that horrid man right in front of me?"

"Yes, ma'am."

Her smile hadn't changed all evening. She looked like she was having one hell of a good time. After she returned his stare for a couple of seconds, she shrugged. "All right, I did understand all of it, but you looked and sounded so pleasant, I thought I might have got it wrong."

"No reason to talk rude in front of a lady."

Her laugh came from deep inside. A man could get in the habit of playing the fool for a reward like that.

"You are the damn'dest man I ever met."

"I love the way you curse. There's music to it when done right. It's a shame so few women can carry a tune."

"In your twisted way, are you trying to reprimand me for an occasional unguarded word?"

"Yes, ma'am."

"I don't take reprimands well."

"No, ma'am, I don't expect so. Training horses and women tries the patience of most men. That's why so few come to be good at it."

"And I suppose you think you're one of the few."

"With horses, yes, ma'am. The benefit from women seldom justifies the time it takes."

Her eyes reminded him again of onyx, hard and black, but showing a tint of red or brown when held up to a strong light. "Where did you learn so much about rubies? Is there really such a place as Moguk, or did you make all that up?" His attempts at teasing humor continued to go nowhere with this woman. She simply ignored him or changed the subject.

"Yeah, Moguk's a real place, eighty or ninety miles from Mandalay, if I remember rightly. When I tire of reading tomato can labels, I read books."

"What kind of books?"

"The kind I can find."

"Are you always so evasive?"

"I'm terribly honest and sincere. It seems to irritate suspicious people like you for some reason."

"Why do you suppose those two ruffians approached me?" The Amazon could change the subject of conversation quicker than a miner could drop tools at the lunch whistle.

He shrugged. "A pretty woman causes people to take notice. Raymond met you at the stage when you arrived and had dinner with you. You went out to the mine and spent several hours. Didn't take a brainstorm to suspect you might own stock, especially since you sport the same name as your late brother. They might have figured to scare a timid woman so they could buy valuable stock cheap. Maybe they thought they could cause confusion in the enemy's ranks. Maybe they just took a chance to try their charms on the prettiest woman in town."

"Everyone in the hotel is talking about them

claim-jumping our mine. John Ely is out of town. What is Mr. Raymond going to do?"

Darnell briefed her about the meeting with Morgan Courtney that afternoon, confident his low tone could not be overheard from the nearby tables. The waiter came by, took their order, and went on his way.

"There's going to be bloodshed then?" Her question might as well have been whether it would rain tomorrow.

"Looks like it."

"Then you need to start being very careful."

"No, ma'am. I started being very careful eight or nine years ago when I left Louisiana. All I need to do now is follow old habits, act normal. You're the one who's new to it, but you're doing just fine. I worry about gun oil though."

"I beg your pardon. What does that mean?"

"You picked a table well away from the windows, couldn't have done better myself. But won't gun oil ruin a pretty green dress? Seems to me it might make a spot and be hard to wash out."

When she didn't answer, he added, "If I wore pretty dresses, I'd leave that house gun in my open handbag and hold the bag in my lap. I wouldn't put it under a napkin."

Nothing could shake her. He saw no tremor, no blink, nothing. He wondered if his guess had missed its mark, but then she lifted her bag from the floor beside her foot. The transfer of the little Colt from her lap back into the bag took place under the cover of her napkin, smooth, casual, hidden.

"How did you know?"

"Guessed."

"Really? You just guessed?"

"We're getting to know each other quite well, aren't we?" He wagged his brows up and down and aimed a waggish grin her way. Her smile never changed, so he allowed his grin to die a natural death. He drew a deep breath and let it out slowly. All right, so she didn't like his sense of humor.

"I found out some things you should know, but maybe Mr. Raymond told you this afternoon." The Amazon stopped speaking when the waiter arrived with filled plates.

Darnell didn't answer. He picked up his fork.

"But it'll wait till after we eat."

When he looked up, he found her looking at him with real amusement. Her smile reached up and included those hard eyes for a change. She had decided to go along with his distaste for mixing business with food, but she made the concession sound patronizing. He returned the smile. "I appreciate every kind thing you do for me."

"Does your prejudice allow personal matters to be discussed?"

Damned if she didn't sound friendly. She didn't make that out to be a condescending question at all. In fact, she sounded unsure, tentative. He chewed, swallowed, took a drink of water, and gave himself a chance to consider. Finally, he took a gamble.

"Linda, you talk about whatever suits you. The sound of your voice pleases me."

The silence following his comment convinced him he'd made a mistake. This would be the last time. Enough. If he kept trying to play Romeo with this icy Amazon, he'd only make a fool of himself. Still, he'd thought it might be worth one last try.

When she finally spoke, her voice sounded unsteady. "I want to tell you about my step-brother."

"All right." He kept his eyes on his plate. Something about her voice told him not to look at her.

"He was almost twenty years older than me. When his father married my mother, he was twenty-five and I was six. My mother died when I was thirteen, and his father died two years later when I was fifteen. Fitz became my father for the next twenty years until someone killed him here in Pioche. He was only fifty-five."

Darnell finally looked up and found her ignoring her food. Her eyes were fixed on him. He carefully placed his fork on his plate and leaned forward to hear, but he averted his eyes again. She now spoke hardly above a whisper. He nodded to signal that he heard and understood, but he feared to do more. Anything he might say at this moment carried too much risk. He knew a wrong word would stop her, and she'd never venture this confidence again.

"Since Fitz never married, and we lived in the same house, someone started talk, and it never seemed to go away."

She stopped again, as if waiting for him to comment, but he didn't dare. He lifted his water glass, keeping his expression one of courteous interest.

"Fitz wasn't like other men." Another long silence followed, maybe only ten seconds, but it seemed to last ten minutes.

"He was the most gentle, generous, thoughtful man ever born. He taught me to ride, to shoot, to dance, everything. He even taught me to cook, but he had to hire women to teach me to sew. He took me everywhere, saw I got the best schooling. Fitz used to laugh with me about how men gave women no decent schooling and then liked to claim they were stupid. He believed an untrained mind would almost always seem inept in the presence of trained ones. He trained me to be his business adviser, taught me bookkeeping."

Darnell chanced another glance and found her looking straight at him. An inner voice screamed caution, so he controlled his expression. She watched him, he knew, waiting for the slightest wrong move, the tiniest facial twitch.

"Fitz loved women, and women loved him. He loved them, but he didn't desire them."

She stopped, and he knew he had to commit

himself. He had to say something. "Was he ill?"

"No, he was a sturdy man, powerful really." Her eyes dropped, and she stared at the tablecloth, but Darnell knew she didn't see it. She drew in a deep breath, like a person about to lift a heavy object.

"Fitz never married, never took a mistress. Someone started talk. Because we lived together, the rumor started that I was his woman. Fitz heard the rumor. Men don't duel anymore, but Fitz beat a man nearly to death with his fists. That display of manly anger only seemed to make more people believe the rumors. People love to be hateful in the guise of being righteous."

Darnell gave up trying to eat. He touched his napkin to his lips, wondering what brought all this out of her. The only reasons he could imagine made him feel a rising sense of excitement. He decided to go right at it. "So your parlor stayed empty, leaving a pretty girl without suitors. The pretty girl's pride got bruised, so she closed and locked the door."

"Yes." The brutal simplicity of her admission came as no surprise.

Brutal simplicity sometimes carried with it a rugged, intimate brand of sincerity. It called for the same kind of reply. "Dig around and find that key. A real man might come knocking."

She didn't answer. That was good enough. She didn't spit in his eye.

He rubbed his face with both hands. His effort to control his expression so sternly had left him with a stiffness around his eyes. "You stung me pretty hard when you said you didn't trust me. That was only yesterday. I know you've changed your mind or you wouldn't be telling me this."

"Yes."

"Why?"

"I wanted to tell you when we went riding, but you distracted me so much I didn't get to it. I find you bewildering at times, and I get flustered."

"Tell me now."

"At first I couldn't believe it, so I waited until I was absolutely sure you were who I thought you were. You used to wear a beard. We are almost related."

"What do you mean by 'almost'?"

She put on that smile of hers, the expression of iron. "My mother was a Fitzpatrick by marriage. Before that she was an Ozuna by marriage, and before that, she was born a Silvana. She was one of your wife's cousins."

"How come we never met?" Darnell thought he knew all his wife's family except the ones back in Spain.

"We have met, but only once. I was very young. We visited in New Orleans once when you were in town. We visited fairly often, but we always seemed to miss the times you were there too. You probably didn't notice the Ozuna name, probably took us for another branch of the Silvana tribe, and that wasn't exactly a mistake."

"Well, I'll be damned."

"I love the way you curse. You must practice a lot."

He kept a straight face. "I don't accept reprimand well."

"With training, you'll learn, if some woman decides the benefit warrants the patience required."

Darnell had to grin else his face would have ruptured.

"I've ruined your meal, Darnell."

"Ruin all the meals you want, Linda, if you always make me feel this good."

"May I talk business now?"

"Talk."

"You haven't looked at the books since you've been here. I have. The last three weeks have been fabulous. We've broken into the best ore in the history of the mine. Mr. Raymond really paid a high price for Mr. Courtney's services."

"Well, I'll be damned. He had plenty of chance to tell me that, but he didn't say a thing."

"He might have been afraid you'd protest and ruin his ability to bargain. But don't be damned yet. Let's wait to see how well Mr. Courtney earns his fee."

"You're shaping up to be a handy business partner."

She met his eye and flashed her iron smile. "Damn right."

He blinked and wondered if it came from a trick in the light. Those black eyes of hers didn't look hard at all.

FIFTEEN

Darnell spent the next morning at the mine with Raymond discussing the situation. They posted guards on the road to stop any attempt to transport stolen ore from the Newlandses' shaft, but they didn't have enough guards to keep food and water from being delivered to the men behind the barricade.

When they settled into chairs at the headquarters building, Darnell said, "Looks like a standoff to me. Could last a long time."

Raymond nodded. "Courtney hasn't said anything except he'll move when he's ready. He told me not to stir anything up."

"Looks like a dozen or so riflemen behind that barricade. That's not something a man wants to charge up against in a hurry." Darnell pulled out his watch.

"You having lunch with Miss Fitzpatrick again?"

"Yeah. Then she wants to go for a ride."

"What? That's dangerous. She can't be riding around like that. Risky for you too, Baynes."

"I told her that at breakfast."

"Thank heaven."

"She said she wanted to ride anyway."

"Forbid it! Tell her you won't allow it."

Darnell rubbed his smooth face. Man has breakfast with a lady in the morning, he needs to start the day spruced up. He nodded agreeably. "Come along with me, Mr. Raymond. I want to watch you forbid it. Tell her you won't allow it. I'll learn how it's done. Didn't work when I tried it."

"This is absurd. We're about to have a war here, and she wants to ride around like she's on a holiday."

"I said the same thing. Maybe you can say it better. Come on. I'll buy your lunch and watch how you do it."

Raymond came out of his chair and leaned fists on his desk. "I'm serious, Baynes. You think this is some kind of joke? We already had one Fitzpatrick killed here."

"I mentioned that too. Maybe you'll have more luck."

Raymond walked to his favorite window and stared out, mumbling curses under his breath. He smacked a fist into a palm a couple of times. "Women should not be allowed to own property. They get arrogant and out of control."

Darnell chuckled. "So that's what causes it."

Raymond wheeled on Darnell and pointed an accusing finger. "Your attitude is irresponsible, sir. We can't have another stockholder assassinated. My God, a woman at that. They'll melt the telegraph wires. I can see headlines in the newspapers all over the country. Hexed mine puts curse on owners. Our stock wouldn't sell for pennies."

Darnell kept his voice level. "Mr. Raymond, the lady has not given me permission to take responsibility for her."

The finger pointing at Darnell seemed to catch Raymond's attention. He dropped his hand quickly. "I beg your pardon."

Darnell waved off the apology.

The little miner snapped his fingers. "Mounted guards, that's the answer. Dawdle over lunch. That'll give me time to send a couple of my guards to get horses. They'll follow you. I hope two will be enough. Do you think two is enough?"

Darnell replaced his watch in a vest pocket and rose. "I'll tell her it was your idea."

"You can tell her for me, in your cheerful way, that I think she has taken leave of her senses."

"Come along and tell her yourself."

Raymond threw up his hands. "I've got to find two men I can spare. Eat slow, will you?"

Darnell nodded, walked out, and swung into the saddle. When he rode up to the hotel, he found Flea already saddled and waiting at the hitching rail. In the dining room, at her usual table, the Amazon sat already dressed in her riding outfit. As soon as he took his seat, she said, "I instructed the hostler to saddle and deliver Flea to the hotel every day at noon. That should save valuable time, don't you think? I don't want to trouble you with saddling and unsaddling her every day."

"All right."

"You don't sound happy. Are you still sulking?"

"I still think it's dangerous right now for you to be riding around the country. This isn't the safest place in the world in the best of times."

"I bought a new rifle this morning. I'd like to fire some practice shots with it today." The Amazon had a grand way of ignoring what she didn't want to hear.

"Mr. Raymond had a fit. He's sending two guards to follow us around. He said to tell you he thinks you've taken leave of your senses."

"I wish I had my own rifles with me, but my trunk was already full. It's lucky I'm tall, you know. There's no need to have the stock shortened or any custom work of that nature."

Darnell gave it up. She talked about what interested her or went deaf. After she grilled him for news about the mine, the conversation at lunch dwindled to nearly nothing. After lunch, once again, she took off for the open desert as soon as she hit the saddle. At least, Darnell noted with satisfaction, she took a different direction from the previous day. No way to tell, but he suspected she'd taken random routes every time she rode. An ambush of such a rider would be troublesome to set up.

She brought a sack full of clanking whiskey bottles tied to her saddle. The two guards stayed about fifty yards behind, and they showed undisguised interest when the Amazon dismounted and blasted away at her glass targets. Darnell guessed she wanted him to ask her where she got those bottles, so he didn't. She probably had a plan to tell him to mind his own business or something of the sort.

Then she mounted and fired several shots from a gallop. Although the range was only about thirty yards, watching a woman in a sidesaddle breaking bottles with a rifle from a galloping horse made a show as good as a circus act. The performance brought whistles and applause from the guards. Altogether, Darnell had to admit he'd witnessed an impressive display of skill. He also recognized a brazen, shameless exhibition when he saw it. Nobody learned to shoot like that without spending hundreds of hours burning powder. The Amazon wasn't above showing off.

He said nothing when they headed back toward town. The silence nettled her just like he hoped it would, and she finally asked, "Well, what did you think?"

"Fancy shooting." He allowed no praise in his tone, just recognition of the fact.

She rode for a long time before she spoke again, and he turned in surprise at the tremor in her voice.

"Well, what the hell. I had to find something to do while the other women sewed things for their hope chests, all those smug little girls who didn't have to worry about being too tall or what nasty-minded people said behind their hands."

"Good thing you didn't throw it away."

"Throw what away?"

"The key."

"Key?"

"To your parlor."

"Oh."

"You didn't make up a hope chest?"

"No."

"Start putting one together. The seat of life rests on three legs, faith, hope, and charity. Giving up hope isn't righteous."

"Are you trying to pull scripture on me?"

"Obliged to."

"Why?"

"Get you used to it. Wouldn't want you to be too flustered at the language if I drag you up in front of a preacher some day soon."

"What a terrible, obnoxious joke."

"Good thing you didn't laugh, Amazon. I'm a sensitive man."

They dismounted in front of the hotel before she said anything more. She turned to him and moved up close to speak in a low voice, but she didn't meet his eye. "Thank you for a lovely ride." She stepped away, unstrapped her rifle boot from the saddle, and marched into the hotel with her rifle tucked under her arm, back straight as ever.

Darnell took Flea back to the livery stable and

rode to the Perlman's freight line. The first thing he saw when he walked through the door was Ruth Prime seated behind a huge ledger book. She looked up, saw him, and sprang to her feet with a big smile.

"Hello, Ruth."

"Gosh, it's good to see you, Mr. Baynes. You aren't mad at us are you? You rode away so fast . . ."

"Nope. You work here too?"

"Daddy hired me this morning. He fired the bookkeeper. Daddy says nobody comes to work around here with a bottle in his pocket."

"Thought you wanted to go to school."

"I am, right here. I bet I'll learn more around here than you'd think."

"Thought I might say hello to your daddy. Where's he hiding?"

"He's coming down the street right now. See?" She pointed toward the front window. "He went on a ride to Bullionville to see how a new man handles the reins. Isn't he one handsome devil?"

Darnell watched the empty rig wheel into the station yard. Joshua Prime sat beside Fane Trampe on the box. Prime jumped down and headed for the station while Trampe began unhitching the mules.

Prime's face lit up with a smile and he stopped knocking dust from himself long enough to shake hands. "Good to see you, Mr. Baynes. And I thank you for sending me a good man. Not much to him but bones and sunburn, but he knows how to handle a team and he's sober."

His gaze lingered for a second on Ruth, leaning against the door watching Trampe with fixed interest. "Young fellow takes a big interest in learning the business, spends his free time hanging around my bookkeeper."

Darnell spoke carefully. "I've known his family for years."

"Yeah, that's what he said. He said he'd druther I didn't talk that around." Prime fixed Darnell with a piercing eye. "He workin' for you too?"

Darnell nodded slowly. "I just asked him to keep awake and let me know if anything interesting happened."

Prime leaned against the counter and aimed a brown stream at the spittoon. "You got any more like him, send them around."

"Gladly."

"I already done some checking up. You asked me to keep an eye open too. I already took a look at our deliveries for the Raymond and Ely. You remember I told you the Perlman boys told me to watch out for our biggest customer, so I wasn't doing you no favor, really."

"Find out anything?"

"Yeah. If somebody's gettin' out the door with your ore, it's got to be somebody at the mill or it's got to be some of the independent freighters who own their own wagons. My drivers get a signed receipt for each load from down there at

Bullionville. They bring the receipts to me. I count 'em up and charge the Raymond and Ely each week for loads delivered. The bookkeeper at the mine says our count always matches theirs. We'll see. I ain't been here long enough to do no collecting yet."

Ruth turned away from the door and said inquiringly, "Mr. Trampe said he's known you a long time?"

Darnell said, "We were distant neighbors back in Louisiana."

She stood waiting for more. Finally, she said, "Well?"

"Well, what?"

"Is that all you're going to tell me?"

"Yes, ma'am."

A hard glint came into her eyes, and she perched herself behind the big ledger.

"Ruth, don't give me a poisonous look like that. You want to know more about that young man, you ask him. Young men like to talk about themselves."

She looked up from the ledger. "I already did. I said it must have been a pleasant accident for him to run into you here in Nevada. You know what he said? He said it was no accident. It was an act of God. Then he acted like he'd bitten his tongue, and he wouldn't say another thing about it. Said it wasn't wise to tell women too much and grinned like a jackass with a straw up his nose. Why do men think rotten jokes like that are funny?"

Joshua chuckled and said, "He's likely saving up his best jokes for tonight."

Ruth turned on her father. "What's happening tonight?"

"He invited you and me to dinner over at that fancy hotel. I think that poor, sunburned boy's smitten with you."

She dropped her eyes, became fascinated with a ledger page, and color sprang to her cheeks. Joshua leaned closer over the counter and said in a prissy voice, "He said you were prettier than sunrise on a clear morning."

Face flaming now, she sent a mortified glance at Darnell, who put on the most sympathetic expression he could muster. She waited until her father turned back from launching another brown stream at the spittoon before she asked, "What did you say?"

"I done told him I shot me a graveyard full of raggedy boys for trying to hang around you without my say-so."

"Is that all?"

"He promised he'd act as proper as he knew how."

"I guess you two are satisfied you've arranged my life just fine."

Darnell raised both hands, palms out. "Wait, Ruth, before you get mad. None of my business, but I got to say this. I tried my dead-level best to make friends with my wife's family, but they'd have none of me. That caused me no end of pain before we got to be friends later on. One of her brothers came close to taking a gun to me. Seems to me this young fellow has the right idea. If your daddy's taken a liking to him, that's no bad thing if you come to like him too."

Joshua grinned and wiped his mouth with a surprisingly clean bandanna. "Actually, he invited me to dinner, but he said he wouldn't mind if I brought my child along."

" 'Child'?"

He stuffed the bandanna back into a hip pocket and rubbed his chin, eyes toward the ceiling like a man searching his memory. "Maybe he said 'daughter'." He stood thinking for another moment. "Now that I ponder on it, I think he said 'lovely daughter.' "

SIXTEEN

A week went by, and the standoff began to become part of the routine. Then one evening a couple of hours after supper, the guard who had challenged Darnell on his first trip to the mine knocked on his hotel room door.

"Mr. Baynes, Marshal Courtney wants you to join him out at the mine. He sent me after you." When Darnell stepped out the door, the young man said, "You might want to bring your rifle too, sir."

Darnell turned back, snatched his Spencer from the corner, and followed the guard down the stairs. "What's your name?"

"I'm Royce Darrow, sir." He paused for a brief handshake and added, "I took the liberty of having your horse saddled and brought over for you."

"Thanks."

They rode in silence through the darkness to a clump of brush near the Newlandses' shaft. Courtney, his two deputies, and five or six other men lounged in the brush. As soon as Darnell dismounted, Courtney approached and extended a hand. "I had an idea today, Mr. Baynes."

"Glad to hear it. What's the plan?"

"Well, I was visiting today down at Carolyn's when she got in a shipment of honest-to-goodness fine whiskey. None of the regular panther piss, tobacco juice, and hot peppers. Real whiskey."

"So?"

"Well, those boys have been sitting behind that barricade long enough to get bored, don't you think?"

"You plan to throw a party?"

Courtney snickered. "Yeah, and it's got to look right, a real accident. I've got me a new driver, a new man nobody up there will recognize. I want them to think he's made a mistake in the dark. He's going to take a couple of cases of that good whiskey and deliver it up there by mistake. I don't figure they'll let him drive off with that whiskey."

"And they'll get drunk. And we'll go up there in the dark hours of early morning, catch them by surprise, and take that shaft away from them. Right?"

"Right, Mr. Baynes. What do you think?"

"Might work. If somebody starts shooting, at least we can have a decent chance to back off in the dark without getting shot to pieces."

"You figure to go along, Mr. Baynes?" Courtney's tone carried a mix of insulting disbelief, challenge, and amusement.

"Wouldn't miss the fun. When's the whiskey coming?"

"Should be along any time now."

Darnell felt a familiar reckless impulse that stretched his face into a lopsided grin. This dandy with his spotless white linen suits had intentionally planned to make him act like a spineless fat cat, had set him up in front of these men, hoping he'd back away from the dangerous part of the scheme. More than one can play that game.

"Let's slide up the hill and see if we can get close enough to hear what goes on."

"What?" Courtney sounded aghast.

"Let's listen in."

Royce Darrow's low voice interrupted. "Mr. Baynes, those boys up there shoot at sounds in the dark. Sometimes I think they shoot down the hill once in a while just to prove they're awake."

Darnell allowed an edge of sarcastic amusement into his answer. "That sure enough calls for a man not to make any noise all right."

He shifted his Spencer to settle it in the crook of his elbow and glanced at Courtney. "No need for you to come. I'll tell you about it when I get back." He stepped out of the brush onto the open slope, moving in a low crouch. He had only moved forward about ten yards when he felt Courtney beside him.

"You son of a bitch." His hissing whisper would have made a rattler blush with envy.

Darnell stopped and dropped to his knees. He turned and leaned toward his shadowy companion, his own cheerful whisper almost soundless. “We better crawl most of the way or they might see us outlined in the town lights.” He crawled forward, smirking at the thought of what Courtney’s white suit would look like after this. If the moon came out, the marshal might as well be carrying a lamp. He had to hold his breath to keep from laughing. Dare a Baynes and get a dare in return. Debts must be paid and insults returned in kind.

They moved up the slope inches at a time, and Darnell stopped twice to let the marshal rest. Sweat ran off him in rivers, and Darnell knew he wore a cruel smile. Town men don’t stay fit, and tension added to the uphill crawling brought such ragged breathing from the marshal Darnell feared the barricaded men might hear it. He felt a stab of anxious concern that they might have had enough sense to put out a man in front of the barricade. He’d never detected any sign of them doing it before, but it would be just his hard luck to have somebody think of it tonight.

They hadn’t. He came close enough now to see the dark line of the barricade. Narrow gleams of light between the wood beams, hidden from below, verified they had lamps burning behind it. He eased out a long breath in a silent sigh of relief. The fools had posted no listener in front, and they sat blinded by light behind their crude fortification. He could have walked up to the barricade and knocked like a Bible salesman.

He reached out and pulled Courtney to him.

"We get any closer we'll have to kiss 'em good night."

Darnell made himself comfortable on the rocky slope and relaxed, convinced all he needed to do to escape notice was remain motionless. No eye could come from a lamplit area and detect him. He listened to the marshal's breathing finally slow to normal. Ten minutes passed. Twenty.

Darnell hadn't enjoyed himself this much in months. He knew full well the marshal's town man life had done nothing to develop his own kind of backwoods, cool-headed patience. Nor did the dandy have Darnell's cozy confidence that the darkness was his best friend. The marshal's nerves had to be drawing tight as rawhide in the sun.

He almost felt disappointed when the rumble of approaching wagon wheels came clearly from below. The wagon came all the way into sight before alarmed voices boomed from behind the barricade. Somebody shouted, "Stop that wagon right there. Where you think you're going, feller?"

"Got a couple of cases of whiskey I got to deliver. This here's the Raymond and Ely mine, ain't it?" Darnell's stomach jumped when he heard Fane Trampe's voice.

Somebody laughed and said, "Ye dumb sod, this ain't . . ." The voice stopped when another shouted, "Yeah, we been waiting for you. Bring it in. We'll sign your tag and you can head for bed." A roar of delighted laughter and snickers followed.

Trampe spoke slowly, a perfect imitation of a slow-witted oaf. "I'm sure glad this is the right place. I'm new around here, and these roads go ever' which way."

The cases came off the wagon to a tune of clinking bottles. Darnell lay close enough to see the men prancing around the flank of the barricade with their musical burdens. Fane had even been clever enough to put out the light on the downslope side of the wagon. The trail lantern on the barricade side blinded the men while allowing the hidden Darnell and Courtney to see like patrons in a darkened theater.

Another voice spoke with stern authority. "Move along. You done your job."

"I got to get a signature from the man in charge."

"Here, give me that. There. Now you and your wagon get off this side of the hill."

"Thank you, fellers." Fane and his wagon rolled cautiously forward, just the right speed for a driver on an unfamiliar trail in the dark.

Darnell came to his feet and strolled casually down the hill, knowing the moving wagon covered the noise he made. He had come near to the dark clump of brush before hoarse breathing told him Courtney was finally catching up. "You crazy fool! How come you just got up and walked off like that?"

Darnell chuckled. "Those boys had all they

could pay notice to inside that shaft. We'd need to blow a bugle to get their attention."

Courtney brushed at his suit. "Damn that crawling around in the dark. I don't want any more of that. A snake could get you before you could spit." The marshal made no effort to hide the relief in his voice. "You think this is going to work?"

"I'd wait till maybe two or three in the morning, marshal. Give them at least three or four hours. That should be just right. I think you got a good chance to pull it off."

When the men rose out of the dark brush to gather around them, Courtney announced, "Hell, boys, I took Baynes here right up next to the shaft, and those sons never knew we were there. That boy who took the whiskey up to them ought to be an actor. He did a neat job. Now, all we got to do is wait. I heard corks popping before we could back off."

The men sat on the ground or paced back and forth in the inky blackness. Of all the nerve-grinding challenges facing men, the most abrasive had to be the waiting and wondering before a battle. Some talked endlessly. Others went repeatedly into the darkness to relieve themselves. Some of the rifles and pistols must have been checked fifty times as the hours crawled past. Darnell watched and listened, sitting quiet and detached, just enough distance away from the group to be left alone but not far enough away to seem unfriendly.

At first, it sounded like a trick of the wind. A moment later, no doubt remained. The sound of singing drifted down the slope from the shaft. The small group around Darnell froze, listened for a moment in breathless quiet, and then burst into choked laughter. Courtney's low command to keep quiet didn't stop the snorts and gasps from men giddy with relief gaining confidence. Courtney announced, "Another thirty minutes, men."

A silent figure drifted through the darkness directly toward Darnell. Darnell stiffened at the lithe and silent movement, completely unlike the other men surrounding him. Only when he sank to one knee and spoke did Darnell recognize the lanky Fane Trampe. "Evening."

"What are you doing here?"

"Royce Darrow came to pay me for delivering whiskey. He said you were out here. I figured to come watch your back."

"Obliged. What did you get for the whiskey run?"

"Fifty bucks, twenty-five before, twenty-five after."

"Dangerous work."

Trampe shook his head. "Naw, those are just poor Irish up there. A job is a job for them. They're just making wages. The mean ones are with us."

After another wait, the singing died away, and Courtney called them together. "We stay apart while we walk up the hill. Do I need to tell anybody to walk quiet and careful? We got to bust in on them like we fell from the sky. Otherwise, some of us might get hurt. If we got to do any shooting, get as close as you can before you cut loose. Try not to shoot first if you can keep from it. If we pull this off, men, you'll have the biggest payday you ever saw, so let's earn our keep."

He fell silent for a few seconds and then asked, "Anybody got any problems?" Nobody said anything. "Let's go then."

They fanned out in an irregular line. The darkness lay so thick nobody could see more than ten feet. To Darnell's sharp ear, some of these men walked as if they wore wooden shoes on broken glass. He thought of a small herd of horses clattering across a slate slope in darkness.

Darnell was the first man around the end of the log barricade. A brief pause at the entrance settled his doubts. Of the dozen defenders, only four were awake, each with bottle in hand, bleary eyes staring vacantly at the unexpected visitor. The inside of the shaft seemed light as day with four lanterns burning. One of the four men fumbled for his rifle, but Darnell kicked it away. The fumbler looked solemnly up into the barrel of Darnell's Navy for a moment, shrugged, and lifted his bottle. The others streamed in, pistols leveled.

Courtney came in last, gaze searching every corner. One of the four men still sober enough to stay awake mumbled something and started to rise. Courtney shot him twice at a range of less than six feet before the man got off his knees. The deafening shots, magnified in the confined space, made everyone duck in a futile effort to lessen the impact on their ears.

Courtney announced, "Don't anybody else try to go for a gun." Even the sleeping drunks had been shocked awake by the sound of shots like cannon in the narrow shaft. "Take their guns and shove them out of here."

Darrow said, "All guns on the floor before anybody moves. Get up one at a time. If somebody needs help to get up, help him. Move careful, men. No need for anybody else to die today."

Courtney, eyes flicking back and forth, an oddly vacant smile tugging at his lips, pointed at the dead man. "Take that one down the hill with you." The shaft cleared as the drunk guards staggered down the slope and the others from Courtney's group walked outside to watch them wobble down the slope.

Then Courtney's jerky gaze settled on Trampe. "What're you looking at?"

Trampe stood relaxed, bony frame slumped slightly forward, staring at the disheveled lawman. He spoke with his lips twisted in a sneer. "Nothing. I'm looking at nothing."

Courtney sank into a tense crouch. "What're you doing here? Who are you? I don't know you."

"I brought the whiskey to these boys. Didn't figure you'd shoot drunk men who laid down their guns. If I'd've known that I wouldn't have done it."

"You got a smart mouth, mister."

"I ain't drunk. You don't want me." Trampe's sneering tone drew Courtney's two deputies back to the entrance, both wearing surprised expressions. Darnell held up a hand, and they stopped.

Darnell said, "We'll be going now, marshal. I suppose you've got work to do posting guards." He took Trampe by the arm. "I've got another job for you, young man." He steered him outside.

SEVENTEEN

Trampe went along without protest. Darnell's big hand on his arm backed by two hundred and twenty pounds easily propelled Trampe's lanky one hundred and eighty out of the shaft and into the darkness.

As soon as they were a safe distance from the barricade, Darnell snapped, "Young fool."

Trampe answered with equal heat. "That coward marshal didn't need to shoot that feller. No call for that."

Darnell jerked Trampe to a halt, released his arm, and stepped close, the age-old bullying, face-to-face move of a bigger, heavier man. He spoke in a low, hard tone. "Grow up. If you want to be a gun man, learn the rules. Rule one, never pull your gun unless there's money in it. Rule two, never pull your gun against a lawman if you have a choice. Rule three, never pull your gun for fun. You got that?"

Trampe stood for a long moment, his lanky frame rigid. Then he relaxed into his usual loose-jointed posture. "Yes, sir." The answer with respectful words but go-to-hell resonance came familiar as sunrise to a man with grown sons.

Darnell felt his own stance loosen. "You scared the water out of me. I apologize. I took liberty, but I didn't want you killed, and I didn't want you on the run for killing a lawman. Seemed to me you'd come out on the short end no matter how it came out."

"No offense taken, sir." The words said forget it. The tone said next time I'll tear your head off.

"I always get impatient when I see my boys make a mistake. Since I've adopted you, I can take liberties. You got to be patient with an old man, but I'll not put my hands on you again. No call for you to put up with that."

Trampe scuffed his feet, a restless, irritated gesture, and looked away in silence for a moment. Then he chuckled and said, "You don't follow the rules either, Mr. Baynes, the way I heard it."

"What?"

"I been thinking about it. Ruth told me you took on a man who treated her rough. No money in that for you. You did that purely for fun. That's how she told it anyhow. She said you didn't care whether the bell rang or fell from the steeple. You broke two of the three rules your own self."

Darnell tried desperately to dig up a reply, but nothing came to mind. Trampe snickered when Darnell pulled off his hat and smoothed his hair. The quick-thinking young puppy had bested him at his own game and now openly gloated about it, an embarrassment that must not stand. Inspiration finally came.

"Oh, it's Ruth already, is it? I'll have to speak to Joshua about that. He may take an interest."

"Miss Prime, sir. I meant to say Miss Prime."

"Sure you did."

"Honest, Mr. Baynes. Ruth just came out by accident, you know, since that's such a pretty name for a woman. I didn't mean . . ."

"Shut up, Fane." Darnell took a step away.

"Mr. Baynes?" Royce Darrow's voice came low as he approached in the darkness.

Trampe faded back, his hand dropping to his hip. Darnell faced Darrow and answered, "Right here."

Darrow fixed his gaze briefly on Trampe and asked, "May I have a private word with you, sir?"

Darrow's habitually correct manner and speech prompted Darnell to respond formally. "Mr. Darrow, meet Mr. Fane Trampe. Mr. Trampe, this is Mr. Royce Darrow, one of the Raymond and Ely guards." Fane stepped forward and the two men shook hands. "You can speak freely in front of Mr. Trampe. He has my complete confidence."

"Very well, sir." He turned slightly toward Darnell and said, "Actually, I'm Chief of Security for the Raymond and Ely, Mr. Baynes. My men call me Captain, a title I earned in the cavalry during the War Between the States."

He shifted his stance to look directly at

Darnell. “Miss Fitzpatrick and Mr. Raymond send their respects, sir, and request you join them at your earliest convenience at the mine headquarters.”

“At this hour? It must be four o’clock in the morning.”

“Yes, sir, an inconvenient time, I must admit, but may I suggest it will be in your best interest to attend.”

“All right. Let’s go.”

Darrow hesitated. “It’s a business meeting, Mr. Baynes. Mr. Trampe might find it tiring.”

Matching Darrow’s formal manner of speech, Fane said, “I’ll just loiter nearby in case I’m needed, Mr. Darrow. I have a mild concern about Mr. Baynes’s safety in view of recent events.” Fane’s answer brought a broad grin to Darnell’s face. He had to resist an impulse to slap him on the shoulder and laugh.

The late-rising moon had crept into the night sky, spreading its brilliance across the rugged slopes. Darrow pulled off his hat to pull a sleeve across his brow, revealing his own wide smile. Darnell found himself liking Captain Royce Darrow more and more. He had a sense of humor even if everything out of his mouth sounded like a line memorized from a book. “Mr. Trampe, if Mr. Baynes wants you there, I’m sure you will be most welcome. This way, gentlemen.” He struck off at a rapid pace across the rocky ground.

The Raymond and Ely headquarters building

sprayed light from every window. Guards posted around the structure walked routes like sentries and challenged them curtly when they approached. Darnell smiled now that he understood the tightly ordered procedures, Captain Darrow's work on display.

Darnell stopped at the doorway leading to Raymond's office and straightened in surprise. The Amazon sat behind Raymond's desk. In front of her, placed in neat array, lay her Colt, a coffee cup, and a tidy stack of papers. Additional chairs had been brought in. Raymond sat beside the desk, dabbing at his streaming forehead with a damp handkerchief. Tom and Frank Newlands sat in front of the desk with their backs to the doorway. At the opposite end of the desk, a man so heavily muscled he seemed to have no neck sat on a reversed chair, arms folded comfortably over the back. A pistol hung negligently from his slack fingers. The size of the man's hand made the weapon look like a toy. His eyes flicked to Darnell and returned immediately to the Newlands, a malignant, unblinking stare.

The Amazon met Darnell with her iron smile. "Come in, Mr. Baynes. Mr. Darrow, a chair for Mr. Baynes, please." Darrow slipped past Darnell and placed a chair near the door.

Raymond said, "Thank God you've come, Baynes." He straightened and shoved his handkerchief into a pocket. The Newlands never moved, sat like statues facing the big man beside the Amazon.

The Amazon, cool as a north breeze, said, "I believe you've met all these gentlemen, Mr. Baynes, except Mr. Haspin Bosca. Mr. Bosca, meet Mr. Darnell Baynes."

The immobile muscular figure twitched an eyebrow at Darnell and spoke, a rumble at the bottom of a mine shaft. "Call me Boxcar."

Evidently Boxcar didn't observe formalities like handshakes. Darnell sat in his appointed chair and wondered what all this could be about.

Raymond, as if he'd heard Darnell's inner question, blurted, "Miss Fitzpatrick," he hesitated before he picked the next word, "negotiated with the Newlands brothers to turn over their Washington and Creole mine to the Raymond and Ely and relinquish all other claims they have against us. They settled for a sum of money, offered and accepted before witnesses. That completed, Miss Fitzpatrick demanded proof of your safety after the raid on the illegal Newlands mine shaft. The Newlands have agreed to leave Pioche under special escort, never to return."

He reached for his handkerchief again. "Now that your safety is assured, Mr. Baynes, I think the Newlands brothers may leave." He finished his last comment more like a query than a statement, and he turned a questioning glance toward the Amazon.

She nodded to Darrow, who was standing beside the door. He stepped outside and someone gave a shrill, piercing whistle. A moment later, a stage drew up in front of the building. She smiled at the Newlands, still sitting as if hypnotized. "You won't forget the terms, will you, gentlemen? If you have trouble remembering, the agreement you signed is written in plain language."

She dropped papers from the stack in front of her into the laps of both men. "If you fail to follow the terms you have signed your name to, you will be making a fatal error. You must do your part to avoid further violence."

Both brothers nodded, Darnell's first proof that the two still lived. He had begun to suspect they were propped up corpses.

The Amazon picked up her Colt, unbuttoned the front of her riding coat, and holstered the weapon. She spoke without looking up from buttoning the garment. "You may go now." They came to their feet like feeble old men and walked painfully out to the waiting stagecoach.

Darnell kept a poker face as they dragged past him. "Seems like you had a plan after all. Why didn't you let me in on it?"

She stood and walked around the desk. "Did you tell me about the plan to attack that barricaded mine shaft?"

"Didn't have a chance."

"Nonsense."

Darnell thought it over. Truth to tell, he could have come back to town and knocked on her door during the hours spent waiting for the barricade guards to get drunk.

He shrugged. "You're right. Didn't know about it myself until after dark. I guess I should have come banging on your door at two o'clock in the morning. I never gave it a thought."

"Join me for an early breakfast?"

"Be most pleased, ma'am. Owl-hooting around all night has given me a big appetite."

The sky grew lighter in the east when they rode up to the hotel. The clerk went around the dining room lighting the lamps when they sat down at the Amazon's table. Darnell wondered if he ought to take that table back to California with him. He'd eaten so many meals off it that it seemed like home.

The clerk said, "The waiter won't be here for another ten or fifteen minutes."

Darnell flipped a hand palm up, accepting the wait.

The Amazon wore a smug expression. "Now, I suppose you expect me to explain everything."

Darnell leaned forward and met her black eyes squarely. The next thing he heard from her that he could interpret as patronizing would be the last he'd tolerate. He walked in. He could walk out just as easy. "Don't strain yourself, Linda. After crawling up and down rocks all night, I'm too tired to give a damn."

She flinched. He saw it clearly. Damned if she didn't look hurt and confused. What could be going on behind that iron smile?

"I said that badly. What I wanted to say was,

may I explain what happened now, or are you too tired?"

Her tone sounded contrite. He listened to the echo in his mind for a few seconds, trying to find a flaw. Couldn't. If she was faking, she had him fooled clear down to the ground.

He gentled his tone. "I'm not tired, Linda, but I got to admit I feel a little cranky. We got behind that barricade and amongst those men dead easy. They were all blind drunk on whiskey we sent up to them. Marshal Courtney hauled off and shot one of them for no reason at all. Seeing that kind of meanness sours a man's disposition."

"I'm sorry. I tried to arrange things before anyone got hurt."

"Not your fault. Still, you got a dose of my bad temper. A man always takes out his bad temper on those closest to him."

"Am I close to you?"

"That's not for you to ask, Linda. That's for you to say."

"I wish to be close to you." She didn't hesitate to think about that, and he caught no hint of sarcasm.

"Your wish is granted. I'm a magic man, Linda. See how easy I make your wishes come true."

She fixed her attention on the table in front of her. "Boxcar is my employee. He's a special agent from the Pinkerton Detective Agency. I hired him in New Orleans before I came here.

Captain Royce Darrow is also my employee, on special retainer, to keep me informed. Mr. Darrow's only condition was that he would refuse to do anything disloyal to Mr. Raymond unless he proved out to be cheating me. When Mr. Darrow came for you last night, he alerted me first that he thought the assault on the mine shaft was coming."

"And you've been arranging all these days to stick close to me so you could squeeze everything I knew out of me."

"Yes."

Darnell nodded, face stiff. This conversation hadn't started out to make him feel chesty, and he figured the worst might be yet to come. This woman made him feel like a spare wheel.

"Mr. Darrow thinks that slim young man is connected with you in some way. I forget his name. He came to dinner at the hotel one night with that pretty girl and her father."

"Fane Trampe."

"Whatever. Is he your employee or just a friend?"

"A little of both, I guess."

"It seems our methods are similar. We both employ secret agents to obtain information."

Darnell nodded again. He had nothing to say.

"I nearly fell out of my chair when you confronted the Newlandses. In one short statement, you cut them down with information Fitz and I spent months gathering. You came out with a stunning intuitive analysis after only being here a few days and without prior investigation. Correct?"

Darnell shifted in his chair and leaned forward. The rule demanded by those who defined good manners was not to put elbows on the table. To hell with it. "We didn't take time to investigate. I didn't like the profit-and-loss statement, so I came out here to snoop around."

The Amazon's eyes never shifted from his face. "I thought so. You're the kind of man who deals with paper records efficiently enough but who prefers to deal with people."

He felt a chill. It cools a man to hear himself evaluated like a something lifted from a toolbox.

She went on, voice level, a teacher reviewing a dull history lesson. "Their mine has not been profitable lately, and that explains their desperate actions, just exactly like you said. I drew up several copies of an agreement to buy them off, offering them enough money to get a start somewhere else. Even so, I offered them less than my analysis of our legal expenses indicated it would cost to fight them in the courts."

She lifted her bag, took out folded papers, and put them on the table in front of him. "Six copies exist, one for William Raymond, one for John Ely, one for you, one for your partner, one for me, and one for filing with the records at the courthouse. The Newlandses signed them all, as did Raymond. I signed also to prove majority stockholder approval if that should ever be necessary."

Darnell picked up the papers and slipped them into his inside coat pocket without looking at them.

The Amazon paused and her brows rose in question. "Don't you want to examine the agreement?"

"Why bother? Deal's done. Fait accompli."

"Don't be angry. I intended to consult you, but the violence last night forced my hand."

"Nonsense."

She flinched again, the tiniest possible change of expression. A flash of what looked like pain crossed her face and vanished behind the iron smile. Darnell decided he faced the most consummate actress he'd ever met. The real Nevada tough at this table wore a feminine riding habit and concealed a frigid, crafty brain behind a carefully protected pale complexion. She sat quietly, convincingly looking at a loss for words.

Darnell leaned back in his chair, forcing down his rising anger, forcing his slack body to conceal his fury. "Water already downstream won't turn a wheel. It's a waste of time to fret about it. Besides, it sounds like you ended the trouble."

The Amazon put a hand on the table in front of him, a gesture oddly like she was pleading. Her voice dropped almost to a whisper. "I planned to consult you today, but you attacked the Newlandses last night. That caught me before I was ready. Boxcar's been watching the Newlandses for days, tracking their habits. I had him go get them. I instructed him to overpower them if necessary, and it was. If you got yourself killed, I decided to kill them both and to hell with the agreement. To hell with everything. If you hadn't walked in that door at the mine headquarters this morning, they'd both be dead now."

Darnell didn't trust himself to speak. He feared to move. She had him flummoxed. He'd have been less surprised if she'd pulled her pistol and shot him. Raymond's shaky voice came back to him, saying something about Miss Fitzpatrick demanding proof he was safe. He hadn't paid attention to that, and he should have. Raymond had almost been chattering, and Darnell hadn't been sharp enough to catch the meaning. He felt like a rabbit staring at a coyote. If he moved, he'd be caught. If he didn't move, he'd be caught. Ask a question — that was it. Ask something to get her to talk until he found his balance.

"How many men have you killed, Linda?" Beautiful. His voice came out steady and a little amused.

"None. I've never made love to one either, Darnell, but I'm confident I can do it."

He sat looking straight into black eyes, not hard black chips of stone now but soft and filled with tears, set in a pale complexion gone full-blooded scarlet.

Darnell lifted a hand from under the table where it was hidden as usual, and touched hers. She latched on, grip tight and strong. He thanked his stars the room was still empty.

"I never courted an Amazon."

"Will you try? Please?"

The twisted rope came unwound. Darnell felt himself breathing naturally for the first time since he sat down with this strange woman in an empty hotel dining room. Even his smile came free and easy.

"Can't seem to avoid it. Been at it ever since I first laid eyes on you. Didn't you notice?"

"It seemed too lucky. I couldn't believe it."

"It's tricky to court a woman smarter than me. Makes a man cautious. I got to admit it vexes me at times."

"Not smarter. Different. You go at trouble like a tough man. That wouldn't work for me."

He looked down at their clasped hands. "Yeah, I got to teach you not to let your gun hand get too occupied."

The iron smile stayed, but the voice came out more like a cat's purr. "Didn't you notice? I'm ambidextrous, Darnell. I shoot equally well with either hand."

"I should have known. Amazons come full of surprises."

EIGHTEEN

Two weeks drifted past, and Darnell contented himself floating with the current.

Linda proved more lively and agreeable with each passing day, and he knew he'd have to make a definite commitment soon. A man couldn't ask a single woman to move to California so he could court her conveniently. Of course, he could do just that, but he couldn't bring himself to it.

She'd taken to showing a special light of trust behind those black eyes, and he couldn't risk damaging that. She'd made it plain her experience with suitors in the past had left a sour taste. Besides, he didn't want to leave until Courtney and his henchmen finished the month of rent-free mining Raymond had promised them for displacing the old Washington and Creole claim jumpers.

The episode leading to the Newlandses' departure left Raymond nervous and ill-at-ease around Linda. He admitted to Darnell, "No offense, Mr. Baynes, but Miss Fitzpatrick scares me so bad my clock stops. If I ever saw a woman ready to do murder, I saw one that night. No bluster. No ugly threats. She just told the

Newlandses they better hope you didn't get hurt. That was more than enough, especially after that Boxcar roughed them up. If I was a Newlands, I'd still be drunk celebrating my escape from that room all in one piece."

When Darnell laughed, Raymond grinned sheepishly and said, "Yeah, you go ahead and cackle. I'll bet she doesn't have to blow out candles. She can look at them and freeze the flame."

One afternoon Linda commented that Courtney might be a good marshal, but he was a poor miner.

Darnell asked, "What makes you say that?"

"Well, he's going to make a fortune, that's certain, but he's only going to get about half what Raymond would have in this length of time."

"Good. Leaves more for us. I need the money."

She turned to him instantly and said, "I have money. How much do you want?"

He patted her cheek. "Joke."

She watched him closely, eyes searching his face. "I still can't tell when you're joking."

"Good."

"Twit!" She leaped onto Flea and raced away. He had a sweaty job catching up.

Then one evening, Darnell looked up to find Joshua Prime standing in the dining room door of the hotel. Prime walked over and stood twisting his hat until Darnell invited him to sit down.

With a quick nod of greeting to Linda, Prime

asked, "You got any pull with Marshal Courtney, Mr. Baynes?"

"No more than anybody else. What's the problem?"

Prime flicked a glance at Linda and hesitated. She turned to Darnell. "Mr. Prime can speak frankly, and I'd like to hear this, but I'll leave if you like."

"Your call, Joshua."

"If you don't mind some plain language, maybe you can help, ma'am."

She continued to look at Darnell. "May I stay?"

"I think he's right. You may be a big help. Let's hear it, Joshua." Darnell winked at her. Linda, in public, sent every possible signal that he called the turn. Only in private did she show her independent thinking. The charade seemed to relax people.

Prime wiped the back of a hand across his mouth, looked around, and lowered his voice. "I ain't sure I got all of this, and what I got may not be right. Anyhow, the rumor going around is that a feller has cut in on a woman the marshal kind of claims. Seems Courtney's spending all his time at the mine, and maybe she got lonely. The word is Courtney's got his fangs bared, but this young fellow has a tough rep, so Courtney's being careful. That may be the real problem."

Darnell nodded. "That can put a man in a bad temper rightly enough. How's that give us a problem?"

Prime wiped his mouth again. "Might not have nothing to do with it. But it might. Anyhow, this afternoon Fane and Ruth was coming back from the store together. Uh, you see, he's kinda taken on the chore of going around with her, just so nobody bothers her, you know?"

Darnell caught a quick glance from Linda. He said gently, "I've noticed they find it easy to walk the same gait, Joshua."

Prime bobbed his head. "Yeah, that's a good way to put it. Well, Courtney said something to Ruth when they passed him on the street. Don't know what it was. Ruth swears she heard him say something but didn't hear no words, and Fane won't own up to what it was. It set Fane off though. He turned right around and knocked Courtney on his butt — uh, excuse me, ma'am. He knocked Courtney to the ground, that's what I meant to say."

Linda, hidden behind her iron smile, said, "It's perfectly clear both ways, Mr. Prime."

"Thank you, ma'am. You're a nice lady. The upshot is, Mr. Baynes, Courtney tried to draw, but Fane kicked his gun away and whipped his ass — uh, excuse me, ma'am — Fane administered a physical beatup on Mr. Courtney."

Linda spoke gently but with an impatient edge. "Quit the apologies. Just tell it. What happened next?"

Prime tried a grin, but it died. "Yes, ma'am. The marshal done got his nose bloody in front of everybody and one of his pretty suits total and complete ruined. He done give Fane till sundown tomorrow to get out of town."

Darnell commented dryly, "Fane rode in on a good horse. He can ride out the same way. He didn't sell his horse, did he?"

"That's what I told him, Mr. Baynes, that very thing, but he won't hear it." He stopped for a moment, and Darnell could hear the man's heavy breathing. "I don't know what to do. That boy's taken with Ruth, and he ain't about to let nobody run over him in front of her. Now my Ruth, who's a regular cool head in ordinary times, she done went sneaking around and got my shotgun out of the cabinet. I had to take it away from her. Says she's going to kill that marshal if he hurts Fane."

Prime looked away, and his hand drifted to his neck. Darnell noticed the scratches for the first time, raw furrows from behind his ears around and down under his collar in front. Prime swung his head back and caught the direction of Darnell's gaze. His eyes were watering and his face twisted. "Yeah, Mr. Baynes, you might as well see it. She fought me for that shotgun, my own daughter."

Darnell asked, "What can I do to help?"

"Maybe you can point a direction I ain't thought of. All I can figure is I got to kill Courtney. Don't see no way out. Fane's got his neck bowed. Ain't never seen Ruth do a cut-up like this. She's done got her mind set on that bony boy. She don't listen to her daddy no more. Might as well holler at a corral post."

Darnell glanced around and found Ward standing in the dining room door. He sprang to his feet to extend his hand to his youngest son. Ward, always diffident in public, shook hands as if Darnell were a business associate and turned toward Linda and Joshua. Darnell introduced them, and Ward took a seat.

"You took me by surprise, son. Didn't know you were coming."

"Sold some horses to a man from Virginia City, Pa. Deal was he'd pay on delivery, so I thought I might drift down this way since I was already halfway here."

"Son, Mr. Prime here was just telling us about a problem and asking if we could help." Darnell told the story, leaving out Fane's name until the very last. "The young man we're talking about is Fane Trampe."

Ward, casual as could be, eyes hooded, asked, "You met this Fane Trampe, Pa?"

"Yeah, son. It's Fane all right. No question."

Darnell enjoyed a proud moment, watching his son's seeming lack of reaction. The boy waited. Knowing nothing about what his father might be up to, he nodded like the news meant nothing much, and he kept his mouth shut.

The other two at the table had no way to read the signals Darnell caught. Ward's left hand gently massaged his right, his unthinking habit since he was a boy when he readied himself for gunplay. People who didn't know him intimately would see the small movement as idle activity. But Ward knew himself, knew his own habits, and he surely knew Darnell would see the signal. Ward probably saw no problem here beyond deciding whether to go after Trampe before Courtney could get him or wait and get him if Courtney failed to get the job done.

Darnell suddenly remembered his last letter to Ward had been sent after his first afternoon ride with Linda. The boy's mind must be in turmoil, sitting at a table with a woman who might be a threat, wondering how trouble for a deadly family enemy could be considered a problem, wondering why Darnell gave a damn about Prime or his daughter. Most of all, he'd shown no reaction to what must have been a stunning surprise, the news that Fane still lived, one of the men who had kidnapped his son, a man he thought dead.

Knowing he showed a perverse streak, Darnell raised the ante, deliberately putting Ward under the gun. "Got any ideas, son?" The Amazon's quick glance nearly singed his eyebrows.

Ward, the picture of indifference, flipped a hand as if bored and said, "Get Trampe out of town fast. Lawmen are queer. Kill one of them, honest or crooked, and they all take offense. They act like you killed kinfolk."

Joshua said, "He won't go."

Ward looked half asleep. "Of course he'll go.

He just needs a place to go to and somebody to go with him."

Joshua's eyes narrowed. "What's that mean?"

One quick glance at Darnell said it all. Ward, accustomed since he wore short pants to speak his mind, had done so at his father's prompting. He'd said enough for now. "Ask Pa."

Darnell put a hand on his arm. "Good thinking, son." Ward showed his "I'll-put-salt-in-your-sugar-bowl" smile. The boy knew his father had put him on the spot deliberately, but he didn't yet know why. If Ward once got involved in saving Trampe, the idea of killing him came a step closer to safe burial in the past.

Darnell took five minutes to explain the Trampe feud with his family. When he finished the story, Joshua's face had gone slack. "I done stepped in it. I'm sorry, Mr. Baynes. I thought you and Fane was kind of friends."

"You weren't wrong, Joshua." Darnell took another few minutes to tell the story of Fane's near hanging and their agreement to work together in Pioche. Then he turned to Ward and added, "He rode onto your property and saw how happy Arlo was, Ward. He rode away without even speaking to him, afraid he'd spoil his brother's good luck in having a home. He swore to God he'd never lift a gun to a Baynes again. I believe him, son. Fane says his oath to leave us alone caused the Almighty to bring me to Nevada to save him from a rope. I think he sincerely believes that."

The Amazon leaned forward, eyes fixed on Ward. "You took in that simple boy, Fane Trampe's brother, after all the pain caused by his family?"

For the first time since he'd walked in the door, Ward showed spirit. He matched the Amazon's stare and said tartly, "He didn't pick his family. Arlo never caused anybody pain in his life, Miss Fitzpatrick. He'll die innocent as the day he was born. His kind is free of sin."

The Amazon sat back, eyelids fluttering as if she'd been slapped, and Darnell chuckled, so proud of his son he would have laughed with a gun to his head at that moment. Linda had no warning, no reason to expect that kind of comment from a young man with Ward's reputation. Nor could she have expected that sudden show of fire, a startling change from the apathetic, languid manner Ward had displayed from the start.

Darnell turned to Joshua. "This all needs to be worked out if we're to help Fane. Otherwise, my son might kill him on sight. We're lucky Ward didn't see Fane before he came to this hotel to find me."

Linda asked, "Would you have tried to kill him, Ward?"

"No, ma'am."

Darnell chuckled again and drew an impatient glance from Linda. He felt a stab of sympathy and rested a hand on her arm. "Linda, after a while you'll know why I laughed. You'll learn you have to ask my sons exact questions or you'll get misleading answers. You can start learning now." He turned to Ward. "Would you have killed him, son?"

"Yes, sir."

"Linda, you asked my son if he'd try to do something. Once my sons decide about something serious, they don't think about trying, they think about doing. Trying admits the possibility of failure. My boys don't think like that."

"You said Fane needed a place to go and somebody to go with." Joshua Prime's gaze hadn't moved from Ward. "What do you mean?"

Ward had dropped back into his indifferent tone when he spoke again. "Mr. Prime, Fane's not leaving without your daughter. Don't you see that? He won't do it, and if he tried, unless I'm not hearing right, she won't let him go alone. I knew Fane when we were little boys. He's not afraid to back off if he faces a bad deal. He's got good sense. Sounds to me like she's a chain around his leg. Did I hear the story wrong?"

Prime paused a moment and then slowly shook his head. "You heard it right."

"All right. If she goes with him, where's he to go? He's almost broke, right, Pa?" At Darnell's nod, Ward lifted a palm. "So he needs a place to go. Otherwise the whole deal scares him to death, scares him so bad he'd rather face gunfire." Ward paused for a second or two. "At least, it scares him if he's worth a damn, if he feels his responsibility." After another pause, he said, "Or maybe I put that a little strong. Maybe he's like me. Maybe just taking on the job of looking after a woman melts the bones in his knees unless he has prospects."

Prime said slowly, "She'd go if he asked her. I reckon there ain't no doubt about that no more."

Ward shrugged. "She's probably ripping his ears right now, but he won't ask her. Bad timing." His voice went into a disgusting whine. " 'Come away with me, love, while I run like a yellow coward.' " He shook his head and resumed his normal tone. "Fane won't do that."

Darnell asked, "You got space for another hand on your place, Ward? It would be a happy thing for him to be near his brother."

Ward froze and went silent. Nobody moved. Ward's left hand rose and covered his mouth. The tips of his fingers gently explored the white bullet scar across his right cheek. Finally he looked at Darnell, "It's not that I don't respect your judgment, Pa. If you say he's buried the hatchet, I accept that. But I don't dare do a thing like that without asking Kit."

The Amazon asked, "Who's Kit?"

Ward's hand dropped away from his face. "That's my wife, ma'am."

"You have to ask her?"

"Oh, Lordy. Yes, ma'am. No telegram or any of that. I got to ask her face-to-face."

"There's no time for that."

"I know, ma'am. This is all moving too fast for me. I can't believe I'm even talking about this. Fifteen minutes ago, if I'd known Fane Trampe was alive, I would have hunted him down."

Darnell said, "I'll offer him a job. I can find something for him in California. Then, later, if Kit agrees, you can hire him away from me."

Prime said, "You willing to come with me? I don't pull no freight with my Ruth no more. Maybe you two Baynes men can do the talking. Maybe she and that bony boy will listen to you."

"Let's go." Darnell came to his feet. "We need to get this done so they can leave tonight."

Linda said, "There's an Episcopalian minister in town. I met him this morning. He's a very nice young man, with a practical turn of mind."

Prime said, "I know him. Know where he stays, too."

"Bring them here." The Amazon spoke with firm authority. "That young minister clears out bars for his sermons. I'll not have those young people married in a bar, surrounded by painted women and drunks."

"*I* was." Ward shrugged, cool as a mountain spring. "With my face fresh sewed up and bloody rags all over a table."

"You got a bar in mind, son?"

Ward glanced around. "No, Pa. This place looks fine. Miss Fitzpatrick's right."

Darnell winked at Linda. "Besides, the timing's urgent. We don't want to be too picky."

Ward had the last word. "I recall feeling pretty urgent at the time too. Hardly cared where I was. I wouldn't have cared if I got married underwater."

NINETEEN

"Where we headed?" Ward asked as they walked out into the dark street.

"Down to the freight office." Prime hitched his gun belt and adjusted his hat. "They'll both be there. She goes over every night and finishes scratching in the ledger book. He's afraid she'll lift something heavier than a coffee cup and die from the strain. Hangs around all the time."

"Want me to go get that preacher, Pa?"

"Maybe we better find out if our plan will work, son. We could all be wrong."

As Prime predicted, Ruth sat on the high stool behind the counter, ledger book open in front of her. However, the pen stood in the inkwell. Fane Trampe's lanky frame was draped over the opposite side of the counter, head close to hers. Ruth's face, rigid with fury, eased when her father stepped inside. Her eyes went to the furrows on Prime's neck, and her gaze dropped to the floor, color rising in her cheeks. Prime said nothing; he simply walked around the counter and put his arm around her. She turned her face against his chest and burst into tears.

"Now, honey, no need for that." He patted her head and held her close. "I went over and talked to Mr. Baynes. We might have figured a way out."

Ruth looked up and saw Darnell standing in the doorway. She quickly raised a hand to brush at her cheeks and glared at Trampe. "Maybe you can talk sense to him, Mr. Baynes. He's such a stubborn fool."

Darnell stepped inside and looked at Trampe's slack frame, propped against the counter as if he'd collapse without it. "Fane, I want you to keep your head. Don't do anything foolish. I brought Ward with me."

Trampe snapped alert, tight as a rope when a steer hit the end of the slack. Darnell stepped aside, and Trampe could now see Ward framed in the doorway. Ward, wearing an indifferent, supercilious smile, said gently, "Unwind, Fane. You'd be dead now if I wanted you. You know that."

Trampe drew a ragged breath. "Well, you see I didn't die after all, Ward."

"I see that. You looked mighty peaked last I saw you. That doctor lied, didn't he?"

"No, Ward, he told the truth as he saw it. He told me he thought I was gone, but I fooled him."

Ruth said, "What is this? I know you, Ward Baynes. I saw you once in Sacramento. You knew Fane before?"

"I'm sorry, ma'am. I don't remember meeting you."

"We didn't meet. I just saw you from a distance. I'm Ruth Prime. Why would you want to kill Fane? What are you two talking about?"

"Enchanted, ma'am. Fane and I went through a bad patch awhile back. It's a thing best forgotten, according to the way my pa sees it. How about it, Fane?"

"I'd be obliged. Some things don't make a man proud."

"Let's let the past lie then. I came down here to bring you and this lady up to the hotel. I'm to stand for a witness, I guess."

Darnell said, "We'll get to that in good time. I came down here to offer you a job in California. I need a man quick, though. You'll need to leave tonight to get there in time, but there's a problem. I only hire married men. Single men aren't dependable."

Trampe said slowly, "Obliged, Mr. Baynes, but I can't leave tonight. I got an appointment tomorrow. Besides, you know I'm not married."

Darnell said, "Well, now, that's a shame. It's a real good job, the kind that doesn't come along every day."

Prime said, "I think you better get married tonight and hit the road. A man shouldn't miss a chance to better himself."

Ward said, "Can't you find anyone at all, Fane? Don't you know anybody who'd have you? That's sure enough a sad thing."

Everyone looked at Ruth at the same time. She met the gaze of each of them in turn. Then she turned to Trampe and said defiantly, "I will."

Prime started toward the door. "Good. That's settled. I'll go pick up the preacher and meet you all at the hotel."

"Wait a minute," Trampe's voice came out half strangled. "Wait a minute," he said a second time. "I got to meet Courtney tomorrow, Mr. Prime. You know what I got to do."

Ward said, "Fane, this is none of my business, but since we got to be such friends all of a sudden, I'm going to put my two cents in. You got a choice. You can get married to this lady here and go off tonight to a good job in California. It rains there, you know, and grass and trees and things like that grow. It's as nice as Louisiana, or mighty near. Or you can hang around this dry rock pile tomorrow and shoot a no-good marshal. Doesn't seem like a big problem to me, unless shooting people is a pleasure you just can't give up. Seems to me the kind of thing a man thinking of getting married should give up anyhow, don't you think? I know my wife frowns on it, and she's got a forgiving nature."

Darnell said, "And the lady might change her mind if you put it off. They're notional, you know."

Ruth said, "The lady will damn sure change her mind."

Prime shuffled his feet and put on a pained expression. "Ruth, I wish you wouldn't . . ."

"I said what I meant, Daddy. Now you hush."

She turned to look up at Trampe, towering over her by a foot. "What do you say, shorty?"

Trampe said, "Last time I went to California I got shot."

Darnell laughed. "That happened in Arizona Territory, not California."

"No, Pa, he's right." Even Ward wore a grin now. "We shot him in California and then chased him into Arizona Territory where he died. Remember?"

Trampe smiled down at Ruth. "I guess I got to remember your three rules, Mr. Baynes. Never draw on a lawman if you have a choice, or on anybody for fun, or unless there's money in it. Maybe I better go to California."

"Me and the preacher will meet you at the hotel." Prime walked out the door and vanished in the darkness.

TWENTY

Darnell looked around the changed dining room with a sense of shock. The tables had been shoved back close to the wall, and rows of sparkling glasses were lined up in front of whiskey bottles. Two bartenders in clean white bib aprons ranged behind the tables, polishing more glasses to add to the neat rows. He counted six men armed with rifles posted in front.

Captain Royce Darrow stepped forward and shook hands. "Miss Fitzpatrick asked me to meet you, Mr. Baynes. She wanted you to approve the arrangements since she didn't have time to discuss things with you."

"How did she get you into this?"

"We have a system for her to get word to me, Mr. Baynes, any time she feels she needs assistance. Mr. Raymond will be along soon. Our guards will accompany the newlyweds safely out of town after the ceremony. All of these arrangements are compliments of the Raymond and Ely Mine."

Darnell wandered around the room. Yes, the Amazon had been busy. She and Ward sat at one of the tables, heads almost touching while they talked intensely about something, but both wore smiles. Good. They looked like they were getting along fine.

The young minister came in and unrolled an oversized document on a table. Darnell drifted over and found himself witnessing signatures on an ornate scroll covered with colored flowers and angels. Of course the marriage certificate would be fancy.

Fane and Ruth were married in a simple and brief ceremony. Ruth glowing and Fane looking as if he'd discovered gold. Darnell finally got a chance to join Ward and Linda at her table. "What have you two had your heads together discussing for the last hour?"

Ward made a careless gesture. "I was just telling Miss Fitzpatrick that you have deep pockets and short arms, like most people with Scottish blood."

Linda smiled at Darnell. "Ward says courting me is too expensive for you."

"Is that so?" Darnell shot a glance at Ward with a raised brow.

Linda's smile never wavered. "He says you'd be more comfortable getting married and going on back to California and doing without all this hotel expense to hang around courting in Pioche."

"You think I ought to marry this lady, Ward?"

"Don't ask me, Pa. I didn't ask you when I made plans. I picked mine. You pick yours."

"Ask me." Her black eyes showed warm lights around the edges.

"You think I ought to marry you, lady?"

"I've been hanging around this awful town waiting for you to ask me. Yes, I think I'll be good for you."

"You came here to avenge your brother's death. What about that?"

"I'm not an investigator. I have hired a few very good men who are still at work on that." Her eyes drifted to Captain Darrow, who stood surveying the room. "I don't think I need to be here."

"Will you marry me, lady?"

"Yes. It's a perfect opportunity to merge two bad reputations, don't you think?"

Ward said, "I asked the preacher to go get another one of those pretty pieces of paper. I see he's back."

"You sure move fast, Ward. You haven't been in town half a day yet."

"Can't stay long, Pa. I got a ranch to run."

"How do you think your brothers will feel about me getting married?"

"About time. We wondered how long you'd fritter around. Used to talk about it a lot. We sort of lost hope lately."

"And you decided right away this lady was acceptable."

"You always liked the Spanish type, Pa. You stumbled across another one of those Silvana girls, but she had to come all the way to Nevada to get you. Tough trip."

Linda smiled. "Yes, tough."

Darnell Baynes looked at his son's hand covering Linda's and marveled. Then he remembered how that boy announced his intention to court his beloved Kit almost the minute he saw her. Ward decided about women at lightning speed.

He eased his shoulders against the back of his chair and scanned the brightly lighted room without seeing it. A man felt a special sense of comfort sometimes when he looked inward and found all kinds of plans and expectations. He didn't find himself empty at all.

He came to his feet. "Excuse us for a minute, son. I need to take a lady out on a dark front porch and kiss her."

AFTERWORD

While I adjusted dates and some of the facts to fit my story, the unvarnished history of Pioche, Nevada, reads like lurid fiction.

The conflict between the Raymond and Ely and the Washington and Creole was, indeed, serious business. The contested mine shaft in this book is based on fact.

Marshal Morgan Courtney qualifies at the top of the list of ruthless lawman of the West. He ordered a competitor for the lady of his favor at the time to get out of town. The competitor responded by shooting the marshal — repeatedly — from ambush. A jury, the record says, deliberated three minutes before releasing the killer. It seems the jury agreed it would have been suicide to face a gunman like Marshal Courtney. The lady in question and the killer left Pioche and vanished from the eye of history.

Shame on you if you drift through Nevada without stopping by in Pioche. Fellow Western writer Jack Ballas and I were traveling with our respective bodyguards and stumbled onto Pioche by accident while headed to other places. Some accidents on the highway turn into smashing good times.